Staking a Claim

Lost and Found Series

Elizabeth Lennox

Copyright 2022
ISBN13: 9798831516029
All rights reserved

This is a work of fiction. Names, characters, businesses, places, events, and incidents are either the product of the author's imagination or used in a fictitious manner. Any resemblance to actual persons, living or dead, or actual events is purely coincidental. Any duplication of this material, either electronic or any other format, either currently in use or a future invention, is strictly prohibited, unless you have the direct consent of the author.

Table of Contents

Prologue

Revenge.

The need for revenge had fueled him for so long, it had become a part of his personality.

Tossing the folder from DP Investigations onto his desk, Callum MacGreggor contemplated his next move. Turning in the leather chair, he gazed out at the skyline beyond but he didn't see the buildings he owned. He didn't calculate the next property he might acquire or the construction needed on his current properties to bring them to the point where he could sell them for a profit. At this moment, his mind was focused on only one thing.

Revenge.

After years, *decades*, of planning and plotting, researching and waiting...soon, he'd gain his revenge. His eyes dropped to the folder. The information he'd just read would give him that revenge. It would take a bit of charm, but Callum had learned to charm early and well. A brutal life had taught him when to be charming and when to be tough. He'd figured out how to weigh a person's priorities and how to use their weaknesses against them. He'd learned how to tell when someone was lying and when they were telling the truth, even if they didn't mean to reveal that information. And an even more powerful tool, Callum had learned how to use the system to his advantage.

He'd learned all of that in the tough, unforgiving streets, fighting for his next meal, barely sleeping for fear that someone would sneak up on him and steal what was his, or worse.

He wasn't angry with the person who had shoved him into that life. That lying, cheating bastard had forced Callum to learn how to survive. Looking around his office, he knew that he'd never have gotten so far, accumulated so much wealth and power, if he hadn't been forced to survive on the filthy, brutal streets.

No, his revenge wasn't because of the loss of his home and the lessons in survival that had been forced upon him. His plans weren't to avenge the loss of his childhood. He was going to punish the person he considered responsible for his parents' death.

Chapter 1

Surprises were few. After years of working twenty hour days, Callum MacGreggor was rarely, if ever, surprised.

But the view in front of him was...surprising.

Flowers in full bloom surrounded lush trees, bushes that complemented the landscape and various textures from unusual plants increased the visual interest. Colors, textures, and scents enveloped him. As he paused, even the sounds were surprising. Birds sang, crickets chirped, and the wind whispered softly through the leaves of the towering trees.

And yet, none of that was nearly as impressive as the woman standing in this magical oasis. As he watched, she reached forward, straining to pull something out of the ground, then leaning back to toss the offending weed into a wheelbarrow. Then she said something. He wasn't sure who the woman was talking to, but nor did he really care. She was lovely!

No, lovely was too tame of a word for her. Reddish blond hair shimmered in the sunshine, her skin turning a soft pink from the abusive rays. She should be wearing a hat, he thought. That skin...it was beautiful and his fingers itched to touch that softness, discover the texture and temperature, know if she had freckles or just alabaster beauty.

Again, she spoke and he looked around, his eyes narrowing behind his sunglasses as he tried to locate who she was talking to. But he didn't see anyone.

His eyes returned to her as she laughed. Laughed? Once again, he looked around. She was gardening. What was funny about gardening?

Nothing! Gardening was mucking around in the dirt. Callum hated gardening and paid a significant amount of money to his expensive gardeners just so that he never had to see dirt under his fingernails again.

Who the hell was this woman talking to? Who was making her

laugh?

Jealousy unexpectedly surged inside of him but Callum tamped it down. Jealousy? That was ridiculous! What the hell could he be jealous of? This woman was his enemy! She would become the tool he would use to extract his revenge! She was the one obstacle in the way of his plan to crush the man who had killed his parents!

Stepping forward, he heard the pea gravel crunch under his foot. The noise caught the woman's attention. He froze as she looked up, the weight of her gaze like a gut-punch, stopping his breath for a moment.

How the hell could she do this to him? He was tough and hardened by life! He'd grown up in the streets, fighting for his next meal, scratching and saving, living in an abandoned warehouse until he had enough money to find decent shelter. And even after he'd saved enough, he'd remained hidden in that warehouse, saving more of his hard-earned money.

Saving it for this moment!

"Can ah help ye?" the soft voice asked, her Scottish accent brushing over his skin like a sensuous whisper as she stood up.

Callum stood there, staring as the woman blinked, her long, dark lashes fluttering in the sunshine.

Hat. The damn woman needed a hat!

He spotted a hat on one of the benches. He wondered why it was pointlessly resting on the bench instead of protecting all of that glorious, pale skin.

With a fury he hadn't known he was capable of, Callum stalked over to the bench, grabbed the hat, and stormed over to the woman. Hiding his anger at her callous treatment of her lovely skin, he handed her the hat, bowing slightly as if presenting a coronation crown. "The sun is extraordinarily hot today," he said by way of an explanation.

The woman blinked up at him, but she accepted the hat. Unfortunately, she didn't put it on.

Grinding his teeth, he snatched the hat back and plunked it on her head, then adjusted the angle of the brim so that it covered more of her delicate skin. With a nod of approval, he straightened and backed up a step.

"I'm Callum MacGreggor," he announced.

The woman stared back at him and he was struck by how short she was. The information he'd been given had put her height at five feet, five inches. That wasn't necessarily short for a woman, but for some reason, this lady seemed smaller.

"MacGreggor?" she parroted, her soft, pink lips forming a soft O in surprise. "As in, Castle MacGreggor?"

Callum nodded sharply. He glanced behind him and, for the first time, noticed the ancient, stone castle rising proud and strong. The gardens around the castle had blinded him to the building, which was startling. Castles were built to intimidate, to show grandeur and strength, power and the financial acumen of the laird and lady.

However, it was the gardens surrounding the castle that caught one's attention. The colors and splendor of these gardens were more astounding and eye-catching than the magnificence of the castle.

He realized that the woman was still waiting for an explanation. "I was born here, actually."

Those full, pink lips curled into a smile of welcome. "Aye?" she gasped, stepping forward and pulling off the hat. Several curls danced at the gesture, but Callum ignored them, focusing on her exposed skin.

"Yes. I was just–"

"Come inside!" she replied, interrupting his explanation. "Oh, it's so wonderful to finally meet someone who lived here before! Ah canna tell you how many questions ah have!"

Callum was startled. He hadn't expected friendliness. Didn't she realize that he was the enemy? That he was about to steal her home from her?

The woman needed a keeper!

And she needed to put the damn hat back on!

When she registered his hesitation, she smiled up at him, her sky blue eyes sparkling, clasping his hand with both of hers. "Please? Won't ye come inside and have some tea?"

He listened, enjoying her soft brogue. It wasn't the harsh accents of some who had lived in the highlands all their lives. Instead, it was just a soft, occasional rolling of her vowels that captured his attention.

She'd already taken several steps, then turned to look over her shoulder. "Please?"

He couldn't deny her request. A cup of tea wouldn't be a violation of his vow, would it? Revenge could be had over a cup of tea!

"I would enjoy that," he finally replied, causing that lovely smile to brighten. And that, in turn, caused his body to tighten as lust, unexpected and unappreciated, surged through him. "Who were you talking to a moment ago?" he asked as he stepped forward.

The woman paused and looked up at him, those pink lips parting slightly. She glanced back over her shoulder at the weed filled wheelbarrow. "Oh! Well..." she stopped and shrugged. "I wasna...I just...the plants." She stopped and looked around, then up at him. "I just give them a bit of encouragement."

Then she walked on, her pace a bit faster now. As she reached a side entrance to the castle, understanding dawned for him. The woman spoke to her plants? No, that wasn't exactly what she'd said. The daft woman encouraged them!

Had he entered Bedlam?

She glanced back at him and Callum came forward, easily eliminating the distance between them. She smiled again, the worry in her blue eyes melting away as she held the old, wooden door for him. "I normally wouldna take guests through this mess," she explained as she wove her way through tools and buckets, some new plastic ones and some that looked to be more than a century old, made of wood and no longer water tight. "But since ye know everything about this castle, you've most likely been down here before." She hurried over to a small sink and washed her hands. "How old were ye when ye moved out of the castle?"

"I was fifteen," he replied, not bothering to explain that he hadn't "moved" out of the castle.

Fiona paused, her hand resting on the staircase handle. "Fifteen?" she repeated, startled by the news. "Why did ye leave? Why did ye're parents force ye to change schools at such a difficult age?"

The tall, impossibly handsome man standing in front of her stiffened and, immediately, Fiona knew there was more to this story than she'd been told. This terrifying man was different from any other man she'd ever met.

It wasn't just his height or the evident strength in his arms and shoulders. It wasn't the fact that he didn't have a slight or obvious paunch to his stomach. No, the flat stomach and lean hips were nice...extremely nice...but that wasn't what distinguished him from the many other men of her acquaintance.

There was a personal strength inside of him. Something whispered to her that this man was dangerous. Her instincts, honed by years of lies and deceit and perfected by a profession that relied upon ferreting out the good, the bad, and the ugly, warned her away.

And yet, she was also oddly compelled. There was something, a magnetic force, which lured her closer. She suddenly understood how a predator hypnotized its prey. This man, with dark-as-night eyes that watched her with an intensity that caused a shiver of awareness to run through her, was more than just a predator.

In that same moment, he reached out and touched her. It was just a brief touch, but Fiona felt it all the way down to her toes. Startled, she looked up at him. Another shiver rolled through her when she saw heat mirrored in those dark depths. Her mouth softened and she felt her stomach twist into knots ...everything inside of her was hyperaware of her femininity and compared it to his tougher outer shell.

He was so strong and powerful. He could crush her!

As soon as her mind worked through that, she stiffened, her spine straightened and she remembered that she was strong. She had power. Years ago, she'd vowed never to let a man hurt her. Too often, men underestimated her.

Never again.

"Tea," she sighed, relieved for the excuse to go up the stairs. "This way, Mr. MacGreggor."

"Please, call me Callum," he said as they went up the stairs.

Fiona cleared her throat and tried to speak, but the stairway was so narrow, he seemed to take up all the oxygen in the small space. So instead, she simply nodded and tried to ignore the odd fluttering of her heart as he came up behind her.

Once she was in the kitchen, she took a slow, deep breath and turned, pasting on what she hoped was a professional, calm smile. "What kind of tea do ye prefer?"

Fiona walked over to the shelf that contained all of her favorite teas. "I have blueberry, raspberry, orange spice, or..." she stopped, peering at the man over her shoulder. But the stunned, almost revolted, expression made her laugh. "Oh my! None of the above, ahm guessin'?"

She watched as his arms, big, muscular arms, crossed over his massive chest. For a brief moment, she was transfixed by those arms. And his shoulders. Oooh, and his height! Goodness, her sleepy little village didn't grow men like this! Not even close!

"Do you need help?" he prompted, those dark eyes dropping to the glass jar in her hands.

Fiona startled, looked down and realized that she was holding her favorite blueberry tea. She gasped and spun around, carefully placing the jar of tea back on the shelf. She'd installed shelves along the wall and kept her tea in large, glass jars so she could easily see when one started to run low. "Right. Tea." She glanced over her shoulder. "Would you prefer coffee?"

"That would be great, thanks."

She smiled and nodded, then walked over to the stove, grabbed the tea pot, and filled it with water. "What brought you back to Scotland after so long?" she asked. It was comforting to go about the business of making tea and coffee. The movements were familiar and eased the strange sensations that were zinging through her stomach.

"I'm actually here to ask if you would sell the estate back to me."

The teapot crashed onto the "eye" of the stove, the lid rattling loudly.

Grabbing the heavy pot with both hands, she straightened it on the stove and turned to look up at him. "Well," she sighed, rubbing her hands along her jeans. She wasn't sure what to say. She licked her lips unconsciously. "Hmmm...I appreciate your honesty, Mr. MacGreggor." She tilted her head slightly. "You Americans! So direct! Ye just come oot and say whatever's on ye're mind, eh?"

He shrugged one of those massive shoulders. "It tends to make things easier," he replied, acting as if he hadn't just rocked her entire world.

"I'm sorry that ye came all this way for nothin' then. The estate isna fer sale." She lowered her eyes, not wanting him to see the truth. Well, her words were accurate enough. The estate wasn't for sale. More's the pity. Unfortunately, Fiona knew that she didn't really have the right to tell him that. She didn't own the estate, despite...well, she *would* eventually own the property. It was her right. She'd fixed everything on this estate, all of the problems, the crumbling walls and broken appliances, the sagging roofs and replaced every one of the missing stones! It had been her money and her ingenuity that had saved the castle and the lands around it, not to mention the small, nearby village, from falling to ruin.

The man's features didn't change. They were still hard and uncompromising. Determined. "In my experience, everything is for sale, Ms. Reid." His eyes sparkled with determination. "I just have to find the right price."

Her stomach lurched and she wondered if he was right.

"Or the right currency," he continued, his tone becoming ominous.

Turning away, she fiddled with the jar of coffee grounds as her mind tried to process his last comment. "Well, good luck to ye."

He laughed and the sound...goodness the sound of his laughter felt like a warm caress. She glanced over her shoulder, thinking to tell the man that she preferred "ominous". Somehow, the warmth in his laughter seemed even more dangerous to her peace of mind.

"I've never relied upon luck, Ms. Reid. She's a fickle lady." She felt him step closer and caught sight of him out of the corner of her eye. "I prefer to use logic and...other...incentives to get what I want."

Oh my, those were dangerous and challenging words. She looked up at him. "I'm guessin' that some of ye're incentives are manipulations, am ah right?" Angry now, she poured the boiling water into the French press where she'd already added the coffee grounds. They'd simmer for a few moments. She turned away from him and reached for her blueberry tea. No need to hide her true self from this man. Disappointment was like a knife, stabbing at her soul. Finally, she'd met a man who intrigued her and he turned out to be just like all the others.

"Manipulation is such a nasty term." His finger reached out and she felt the singe of his touch along her neck as he pushed a lock of hair off her shoulder. "I prefer to use other incentives. Generally, both parties in my negotiations walk away with something that they want and need."

Her eyes briefly flicked over his chest, more visible now that his arms weren't covering his rippling muscles. "So ye're not eh bully?" she asked, her tone indicating that she'd already made up her mind before he even answered.

"Oh, I've been known to use appropriate pressure when needed," he countered. "But I doubt that will be necessary with our negotiations."

She almost laughed, but not out of amusement. "Don waste ye're charm on me, Mr. MacGreggor." Her gaze drifted over his chest before lifting to glare into his dark eyes. "Ye might be handily done up with all of those mighty muscles, but I'm made of sterner stuff."

He grinned and the light in those eyes burned hotter. "Excellent. I love a challenge. What's the point in winning when one doesn't have to work for it?"

Fiona had no idea how to reply, so she settled on a perfunctory eye roll, then spooned her tea leaves into the tea infuser, snapping it shut and practically shoving it into the boiling water of her cup. "Wonderful! Another man who thinks he can best me." She sighed with exasperation. "Better men then ye have tried." She nodded to his empty cup and the still simmering French press. "Pour ye're own coffee and let's get this over with, eh?"

He chuckled. "Many of my friends probably consider me to be a trial as well." He poured the coffee into the mug she offered, then looked up at her. "Trust me, I have many uses."

"Fiona!" another male voice bellowed, followed by the slamming of a door.

The sound caused her to close her eyes in frustration and she valiantly tried to stifle a groan.

"A friend of yours?" the giant man beside her asked.

She pressed her thumb and forefinger to the bridge of her nose, trying to stave off the incoming headache. "Nay."

Dropping her hand, she sighed and picked up her cup of tea. "I apologize, Mr. MacGreggor. Aye'll need te give ye the tour of the castle another day."

"Is there anything I can do to help?"

She shook her head, but there was something comforting in his offer, almost a reassurance that this man really could fix her problem.

"Fiona!" the voice called again. "I know ye're in here luv!" Soft laughter floated through the air as they turned the corner to the great room. Then they heard, "Cause ye never leave this bloody awful place!" This last was muttered under the intruder's breath and wasn't stated with any sort of humor that might mitigate such harsh words.

Fiona blushed, glancing up at the man standing too close, hoping against hope that he hadn't heard the criticism.

He had. Mr. Callum MacGreggor cocked an eyebrow with obvious curiosity.

That was ridiculous, she told herself. First of all, she didn't need comforting. She'd dealt with this particular problem all her life. Secondly, she didn't want a man as vital and strong to know that she was basically a home body. It was true. She adored her home, the peace and tranquility of the easy days and soft nights surrounded only by her plants and the occasional visit into the village.

The man trailing behind her seemed so vital, so powerful and alive. He probably never stayed home at night to read a book. She doubted that he ever took a moment to pause in the morning to enjoy a cup of tea out on the stone patio, listening to the morning birds. Or maybe just sit on the swing on a warm, summer evening to listen to the crickets sing.

No, this man probably haunted night clubs in New York City. He probably had women hanging on his arm most of the time. And a different woman in his bed every night. He most likely loved the thumping, driving beat of loud, chaotic music or the thrill of a series of social events where he could talk and discuss events, books, or politics with world leaders or corporate powers.

She snuck another peek at him, revising her mental evaluation. This man was a corporate power. The expensive clothing and the hard edge to his features warned her that he was one of the elite in the corporate world. He didn't take orders, he gave them.

Shivering, Fiona tried to ignore the thrill at that realization. His power wasn't an allure, she reminded herself. If anything, that power, that predatory instinct she could see smoldering in his eyes, should be a deterrent. It wasn't a positive, it was definitely a negative aspect of his personality.

At least, that's what she was trying to tell herself.

Sighing, she turned the corner and pasted a bright, welcoming smile to her face, reminding herself of her ultimate goal.

"Good morning, Father. I thought ye had a big party in London tonight. What brings ye home so soon?" As if she didn't know, she mentally grumbled.

Callum watched as the man he'd loathed for more years than he could count, pulled his hand away from an ornately decorated box. Obviously, the bastard had been peering inside. It looked to be over a hundred years old, with gold leaf decorating the outside, and a large emerald surrounded by diamonds on the lid.

He sifted through his memory, trying to remember where he'd seen that box. The wood looked as if it might splinter at the slightest touch, only being held together by the gold leaf on the top and sides. The emerald had to be at least six carats and the diamonds around it had to be at least one carat each. Since there were over ten diamonds, he knew that the box was worth more than the price of most American homes.

He'd seen that box somewhere before, but he couldn't quite place it.

Callum blamed that fault on the man smiling at the woman with the previously pale skin and gorgeous hair. The skin was definitely tinged with pink now and her hair was a riotous mess. And yet, he still thought that she looked stunning.

"You've been out in my garden again, haven't you?" the intruder asked, pulling away moments before he would have hugged Fiona. "Darling, you know how much I hate it when you muck about in the dirt. Why don't you hire someone to do the dirty work?"

Because hired help rarely loved a space as much as an owner, Callum silently answered for her.

"Because I love my garden, Father. Ye know how much I love digging and making things grow."

Her accent was less obvious now and Callum wondered about that.

The man looked over Fiona's shoulder, spotting Callum and he perked up. "Ah! You have a new beau!" He chuckled, as if he'd made a hilarious joke. "I have to say that I like this one much better than that cowperson you've been seeing."

Callum watched with fascination as Fiona blushed again. This time, her reaction wasn't caused by passion, but by embarrassment. Or perhaps anger? He wasn't sure.

"Father, his name is Angus, as you very well know. And while he's very sweet, I'm *not* dating him."

The man didn't look away from Callum. Two men, both predators but in different ways, both sizing each other up.

"Yes, luv. Whatever you say."

The man's accent wasn't nearly as thick as Fiona's. It sounded like the ass was trying to hide his Scottish heritage and that was yet another indication that he was a complete fake.

"Are you going to introduce us, darling?" The accent was now decidedly British, not a trace of a Scottish brogue.

Reluctantly, Fiona turned, ready to make the introductions.

"Father, this is Callum MacGreggor." She opened her mouth to explain who he was and why he was here, but Callum suddenly realized he didn't want that information shared.

So he stepped forward and extended his hand. "And you are Duncan Reid, correct? It's a pleasure to meet you."

The man puffed up like a lion fish, obviously eager to impress.

"Yes! Yes I am! And this," he spread his arms wide, palms up, "is my oasis! Would you like a tour?"

Fiona opened her mouth to explain that she was just about to do that, but closed her mouth again with a quiet sigh. Callum grasped that there was something off here. There was no affection between father and daughter. That previously non-existent protective instinct reared its ugly head inside of him.

"Thank you, but I've already taken up too much of Ms. Reid's time." Callum paused to set the mug of untouched coffee down on the table beside the sofa. "I'll be on my way."

Callum turned to Fiona, seeing the confusion in her eyes as he took her hand in his. Squeezing her fingers lightly, he said, "We'll discuss that other matter another time."

He kissed her knuckles in an old fashioned gesture, not sure why he'd done so. It just felt...right for some odd reason. "Good day, Ms. Reid."

And then he left the castle through the heavy front door.

Walking out to his car, he wondered about the softness in those hazel depths...was that appreciation?

Callum could tell there was more to this situation than he'd realized.

Fiona watched the man walk out through the front door and something inside of her cracked. She didn't understand her reaction to the man, but suspected that he would be vitally important to her future.

Even if that reaction didn't make sense, she didn't have a chance to consider it and mull it around in her mind, to make sense of her thoughts. Instead, she turned to face her father.

"What brings ye home so soon? Ah saw ye only three weeks ago, Father."

Duncan Reid chuckled and walked pseudo-casually over to the sideboard, pouring himself a large glass of scotch. "Ye dinna think I came home just to see me one and only daughter?" His Scottish accent was back in full force now.

She snorted and turned away, retrieving her blueberry tea and collecting the abandoned coffee mug. "What's the *real* reason?"

Duncan followed her into the kitchen, but Fiona suspected that her father was examining the rooms they passed through, looking for changes. He wouldn't find any. She'd learned her lesson years ago. She never acquired anything new without hiding it away in her bedroom, an area of the castle that her father never bothered to venture into. Not to mention, she'd installed a safe in her bedroom suite. And that safe was hidden from everyone. No one other than herself and the person who had installed the large safe knew that it was there, so her father had no reason to look for it. Inside that safe, she kept all of her precious possessions as well as any cash she might need. She'd learned a long time ago that her father didn't stop his thieving ways around his daughter. Any cash left lying around, even if that "lying around" was in her wallet, was stolen by her disreputable father.

Some might assume that her father came home to check on the health and welfare of his only child. But they would be wrong. Duncan Reid didn't give a damn about Fiona. From experience, Fiona knew that there was only one reason that her father came home.

Money.

He must have run out of money again and was here to coerce her into providing more. Or the man owed a large sum to someone, again. In which case, Duncan was here to manipulate her into paying off his debt.

Fiona dumped the coffee into the large, porcelain sink, then turned to face her father, waiting to hear what ridiculous lie he was going to tell her next.

The man didn't disappoint. "I heard an interesting rumor about a new start up that sounded promising," he explained, following her into the kitchen.

"Oh really?" she asked, trying to smother the sigh of frustration lodged in her throat. If Duncan suspected that she knew what he was up to with these "rumors", he'd stick around and try to charm her into changing her mind about the value of his gossipy information. But Fiona, and her father, knew that his remaining here in the village, or more specifically, here at the castle, would only irritate her further.

No, it was better that the two of them play their roles properly.

So instead of telling her father that she no longer believed his ridiculous "rumor" information, she turned and asked, "What's this latest venture about then?"

He rambled on about a start up in Manchester. He said words such as "solar energy" and "wind turbines" and combined those terms with return on investment and doubling their income as soon as he knew more about the company.

Fiona sighed, mentally shaking her head. She knew exactly which company he was talking about and had already dismissed the start up as a fraud. Okay, not exactly a fraud, but the men trying to start this particular company were putting all of their hopes into a pipe dream. The men were trying to raise enough capital to start up their business, but they had no business plan, no experience raising capital, much less knowledge of installing wind turbines or solar panels, and both men had been fired from their previous jobs at a car mechanic's shop only six months ago for stealing parts and reselling them online. They'd been caught, but their trial dates weren't for another three months due to the backlog in cases currently going through the court system.

From what she'd been able to gather from her sources, the two men genuinely thought they could make a go of it in the renewable energy industry, so they weren't actually trying to steal money from potential investors. But in Fiona's opinion, they were going to fail for multiple reasons and it wasn't a good idea to encourage stupidity. There was no way she would ever invest in a company that didn't have the technical or operational knowledge to actually build a successful business.

Speaking of grifters, she thought and turned to face her father. "How much do you think it will take to ferret out more information on the startup?" she asked, playing the game that she and her father had perfected over the years.

He leaned a hip pseudo casually against the kitchen countertop, running his thumbnail along the edge. She knew that he was trying to pretend like he was calculating a number, but Fiona had known her father too long. She'd watched him play this game her whole life, long before she knew the ins and outs of financial investing. In fact, it was most likely because of his antics that she'd learned to differentiate between a good investment opportunity and the liars and fakers of the world. She'd watched him scam and grift his way through "clients" so often over the years, that she knew exactly when he was hoping to scam her and when he was being genuine. She could count the seconds before he'd speak.

Five...six...seven and...!

"I think I should visit Manchester," he announced, right on cue. "I think the company is worth the looksee and, perhaps an investment sum from you would encourage the boys trying to make a go of the effort."

"I don't believe that I have that much influence in this world," she scoffed, turning to sip her blueberry tea. Unfortunately, her favorite blend didn't soothe her the same way it normally would. The image of a strong, hard jawline and deliciously broad shoulders popped into her head.

Damn that Callum MacGreggor! How dare he interfere with her life like this!

"Sure you do, my dear!" her father chimed in and Fiona realized that she'd lost track of the conversation. Another point against the man in question, she thought with increasing ire. "When word gets out that you've invested in a company, the rest of the world listens! You're brilliant at finding the great deals, the new ideas and innovations!" He chuckled, placing a hand on his chest. "I am just honored that you allow me to assist you in your efforts."

Again, she stifled the urge to roll her eyes. He was laying it on a bit thick at the moment.

"I'm a bit short on funds lately," she fibbed. Fiona was never short on funds. She worked long hours to ensure that never happened. She'd experienced desperate poverty at this man's hands and she'd vowed early on never, *ever*, to get herself into that situation again. Hence, her investment strategy was about knowledge and careful understanding of the stock markets and international investments. She was a very wealthy woman now because of her abilities, caution, and careful planning.

Not that her father would ever know that. If he ever did...Fiona shuddered at what he might do, how he would treat her, if he ever discovered her true net worth.

He reached out to pat her shoulder. "We can talk about this later." He took a long sip of his scotch. "Why don't we spend a bit of time together?"

Oh, he was good! Fiona almost laughed. How many fathers extorted their daughters with the threat of spending time with her to wheedle money from her?

But she was up to the challenge. She smiled sweetly and, without batting an eye, replied, "I'd love that! You are always hurrying off to London or Paris or some other exotic locale. It would be lovely to have you to myself for a bit."

His eyes narrowed slightly, grasping where she was going with her comment. But the man rallied quickly. "Maybe we could do a bit of fishing?"

Fiona almost gagged. He knew how much she hated fishing. The hooks terrified her and the idea of yanking a poor, unsuspecting little creature out of the depths made her want to cry.

But she blinked back her horror and nodded. "That would be wonderful!" He loved to fish and thought he'd gotten her with that threat. But Fiona had tricks up her sleeve. "I don't think I'll fish though. You remember how bad I am at holding the fishing rod." The last time they'd gone fishing, she'd caught something on her line and immediately screamed, dropping the expensive fishing rod he'd bought only the day before. He'd yelled several choice expletives as he'd raced into the icy cold water in a vain attempt to recapture the fishing pole.

"Yes," he replied, nodding his head as he rubbed his chin, obviously considering his next gambit. In a flash, his features cleared and he clapped his hands. "Well, it doesn't matter. We'll find something fun to do together over the next few days! We'll have lots of father daughter conversations and maybe I can finally teach you how to play poker."

Fiona couldn't stop her burst of laughter. Poker? He was going to teach her how to play poker? Oh, she'd relish that lesson!

"I'm sure that we'll find some time for that," she assured him, mentally shifting her schedule so that she could sit down with him and see what he did when he played poker. "Let me know how long you plan on staying this time around. You might need to hit the grocery store though. I don't keep a lot of food in the house now that it's only me living here."

He'd already turned to make his way out of the kitchen, probably heading back to the living room for another round of scotch.

"Why would I need to go grocery shopping?" he demanded, outraged at the very idea of having to get his own food supplies. "Why can't Lydia do that? She has to make something for dinner tonight. She should already have planned for dinner!"

Checkmate, Fiona thought with petty satisfaction. She turned away so that her father couldn't see the triumph in her eyes. Lydia was their former housekeeper and cook. The woman had loved cooking and had spoiled Duncan whenever he deigned to stay at the castle. "Lydia retired, Father."

He stared at her for a long moment, but when Fiona didn't continue, he prompted, "And?"

She turned to look at him, her features bland, but her eyebrows raised in question. "And...what?"

"And...!" he snapped, "who did you hire to replace her?"

Fiona shrugged. "No one," she said easily. "As you've repeatedly told me over the years, this is your house and you alone command it. I only live here." She took her tea and headed out the door. "Call the employment agency and let them know that you'd like to interview cooks for when you are in town. I'm sure that they can send several potential candidates around for your consideration in a week or two."

"A week or two?" he huffed. "Who is going to cook for me in the meantime?"

Oh, the gall of the man! He truly expected to be waited on whenever he came home! Fiona shrugged, trying to hide her resentment. "I guess you'll have to, Father."

He humphed a bit more, obviously outraged at the idea of cooking his own meals. Which begged the question – who cooked for him when he was staying in her London flat? She paid the rent and utilities. The superficial reason for him living most of the year in London was because Duncan claimed to be better able to find her good investment opportunities when he lived in the city and could "hobnob" with the "right" people, as he so snobbishly explained.

But the reality was that he was horrible at finding good businesses in which to invest. She maintained the arrangement simply because he preferred living in London, but didn't have the funds. She provided the funds for him to stay in London only because she liked living here on the estate. The castle was her home, her sanctuary, and her inspiration. She worked on her investments and researched various enterprises that she thought could be viable businesses. And she gardened whenever she wasn't working.

In other words, she paid for him to live in London because she didn't want him interfering in her life here at the castle. He preferred living in London because the posh address gave him the panache he wanted so that he appeared to be the aristocratic-man-about-town.

It had worked out for both of them for years now. Ever since she'd discovered her love of investing and he'd realized that he could live off her efforts, they'd lived apart, both of them relatively happy with the arrangement.

However, Fiona had been considering some changes to their unspoken agreement lately. She hadn't said anything to her father yet, because she hadn't figured out how to get him to sell her the castle. But she was working on a plan.

Chapter 2

"Hello Arthur," Fiona greeted the owner of the local pub. "How are you tonight?"

Arthur's face lit up at her greeting. Quickly, he wiped his hands on a clean towel and hurried around the bar, his arms outstretched as he laughed, hugging her tightly. "Fi, luv! It's been over a week since ye came 'round! Where ye been, darlin'?"

"Fi!" several other villagers called out, pausing from their meals to wave in greeting.

Fiona blushed, grateful for the dim lighting in the pub that hid her pink cheeks. "Oh, I've been busy working in my garden," she explained.

The man chuckled, shaking his head. "Among other things, eh?" he teased. "Come on over here and set yerself down, hiney! I'll have Sorcha bring ye out a big bowl o' stew. Will that work for ye?"

Fiona smiled at the idea. "Absolutely! Sorcha makes the best stew in..." she froze when a large man took the stool next to her, leaving her momentarily speechless. "What are yoo doing here?"

The man's big shoulders briefly brushed hers, causing her heart to accelerate rapidly. "I have to eat."

She blinked up at him, once again startled both by his size as well as the aura of intensity and power that emanated from him. It was overwhelming and...and irritating!

However, Fiona didn't have time for this. It didn't matter that he made her heart speed up and her lady parts make themselves known. She had plans! And this man, with all of those yummy muscles and dark, enigmatic eyes, could not be allowed to mess up those plans!

Fiona tamped down on her resentment, trying to play nice. "Well, that's good," she replied, scooching her stool over slightly so that she didn't feel so crowded by his obnoxiously broad shoulders. "Arthur and his wife make the best stew in the region. But..." she glanced around, wishing she could tell him to go sit elsewhere. Regrettably, all the other tables were filled. Not only that, but several of the residents were glancing towards her and the strange man who had invaded their village. They were trying to be surreptitious about it, but their nosiness was rather obvious.

"Are they all staring at us?" he muttered, leaning closer, his lips barely an inch away from her ear. He was so close that his breath shifted the soft hair by her ear.

Turning away and trying to lean as far as she could, Fiona nodded. "Yes. They are good people. Just–"

"Curious," he supplied, finishing her sentence for her.

"Exactly," she replied, smiling and more than slightly relieved that he understood.

"What do they expect will happen if we eat dinner together?" he asked, amusement lacing his tone.

She sighed, her shoulders sagging slightly. "I suspect that someone will mention our presence here tenight to Bernard and," she paused, her features brightening. "And that will be that!" She laughed at the possibility and, actually leaned in closer. "Oh, that would be a bonny eventuality, now wouldna it?"

He lifted one dark eyebrow. "Are you telling me that I'm te be your fake boyfriend for the evening in order to discourage some other fella?"

She grinned, nodding emphatically. "Would ye mind?" She noticed a very slight brogue in his words now. That made sense since this man had been born here. Had he purposely tried to suppress his accent before?

He shifted on the stool so that he was facing her more directly. "That depends."

Despite the warnings screaming in the back of her mind, Fiona couldn't help but be charmed by the man's engaging and mercurial smile. "You wouldn't help out a damsel in distress?"

He chuckled, shaking his head. "If there was a damsel in distress nearby, I'd certainly offer my aid. But we're talking about ye now, weren't we?" His dark eyes shimmered, the color almost chocolate in the dim light of the low-ceilinged pub before lifting once again to look into her haze gaze. "And you're too strong, too feisty, to ever be in distress."

Fiona's heart thudded. Those words were like the finest wine, making her head spin with happiness.

"Now ye're just flatterin' me!"

Arthur arrived with two bowls of steaming stew as well as a loaf of crusty bread and side of rich, creamy butter. "Is the man botherin' ye lass?" he asked, giving Callum the evil eye.

Fiona glanced sideways at Callum, considering how to answer. Callum merely lifted a dark eyebrow, daring her.

She laughed at his expression, shaking her head. "Nay," she replied to Arthur and instantly the man relaxed. "He's an old friend, Arthur."

The pub owner nodded, relieved at not having to deal with a man twice his size. "Well, ye let me know if things change, eh?" he said, looking directly at Callum. "He might be a big en, but between the rest o us, we could take him down fer ye, darlin'."

To his credit, Callum didn't laugh. At least, he held off on releasing the chuckle until Arthur had moved down to the other end of the bar.

"Ye're bad, mon!" she hissed, turning back and taking the large spoon. She took a bite of the stew, then sighed with happiness. "This is the best stew around!"

Callum watched as Fiona took a taste of the brown stew. Keeping his features steady, he took a bite of the stew and swallowed. It wasn't horrible, but it took all of his concentration to keep himself from gagging. To cover up his reaction, he grabbed a large chunk of the bread, hoping it would wash down the taste.

It didn't.

He hurriedly sipped the ale. It helped, but only slightly.

"Come with me," Fiona commanded, then stood up and placed the wooden board with the bread and butter on it on top of her bowl of stew. With her other hand, she grabbed her pint of ale and headed towards a corner table that was now free. She jerked her chin towards the seat facing the wall and she slid into the bench that faced the rest of the pub. "This should help."

Callum didn't understand what she was doing, but he sat. When he looked up, he realized that the other patrons in the pub couldn't see his face now. Relieved, he picked up his spoon and stirred the stew, wondering how long it would take him to finish the rest.

"Eat the bread," she ordered, pushing the board, loaf, and butter towards him. "Leave the stew and tell me why you don't like it."

Sighing, he dropped the spoon. "Just bad memories," he replied, not willing to go into the details of his past.

She glanced up at him, her eyebrows lifted in inquiry. "That's it? I'm aboot to save ye from a beating by a whole hash of villagers and all ye can say is 'memories'?"

Rubbing a hand over the back of his neck, he looked around. "Just...as a kid, I had to eat a lot of stew. I ate it rather than starve, but ever since then, I can't stomach any kind of stew."

She nodded, slowly understanding. "I get that."

"You do?"

She shrugged and took another large spoonful of her own stew. "Absolutely. When I was a kid, my mother made fish for dinner one night. I got a horrible flu bug that night and..." she grimaced. "Well, suffice it to say that, ever since then, I canna eat fish."

He nodded, grateful for her understanding.

Fiona gestured to the bowl of stew in front of her with her spoon. "Just let me finish this bowl off and ah'll make a credible dent in yours. We can switch bowls, so Arthur thinks it's me that didn't finish the stew." She looked up at him, a stern expression in her eyes. "Never offend the bartender!"

He laughed and took another chunk of bread, liberally smearing it with the fresh butter. "I appreciate your help."

She took another bite, closing her eyes as she savored the complex flavors. "Not a problem," She opened her eyes and glared at him. "But you owe me!"

He nodded. "Agreed." He took a bite of the bread and groaned. "Oh, this is *really* good bread!"

"Good ale too, eh?" she offered, looking at his glass that was more than halfway gone already while she'd barely sipped her own.

"Excellent ale," he replied and downed the rest, then casually exchanged glasses with her so he now had a nearly full pint of ale. "Thank you!"

"Hey!" she exclaimed, glancing at the glass. Then her eyes moved furtively towards the others in the pub, noticing that several of them had glanced in her direction. Quickly, she lowered her voice. "That was *my* ale!"

He shrugged, lifting the glass out of her reach when she tried to grab it. "You don't like ale."

Fiona looked nervously around, and then glared at him. "How do you know I don't like ale?"

"Because you sip it carefully," he replied, leaning forward on his elbows. "And you cringe with every sip." He nodded, indicating the bowl of stew. "Better eat up."

She rolled her eyes, but took another bite of the delicious stew. "Okay, so I'm not in love with ale. I just..." she sighed and took another sip. "Ay need something to drink with my meal and Arthur would be offended if ay don't love his beer or ale." She tapped her spoon on the edge of her bowl. "It seems that drinking ale is a Scottish sport."

He nodded, cradling the ale. "Same with Americans. But you don't have to love beer. I'm sure that Arthur has some wine that you could drink instead."

She groaned. "Nay." She shook her head sadly. "Ah'm afraid that ah'm a bit of a wine snob. Ah have a delicious, secret supply of wine at the castle, but Ah couldn't..." she stopped, looking up at him with surprise. "Well, ay'm savin' the good stuff fer a rainy day."

He eyed her curiously. "That wasn't what you were going to say."

Fiona cursed silently, then took another bite of the stew. "Why are ye *really* here?"

He opened his mouth to reply, but his answer was interrupted by the door to the pub slamming open and a loud, "Hello everyone!"

Fiona groaned. She'd come here to the pub to escape her father's presence. Damn the man! Why couldn't he just tell her how much he needed and head back to London! He hated being here in the village!

Although, maybe he didn't hate it quite so much. The villagers all cheered his arrival, greeting him as if he were a returning war hero. It was nauseating to watch. Her father went from table to table, shaking hands, kissing the cheeks of the ladies, flirting with the older women, and showing overt respect for the younger, married ladies. A few times, she caught her father eyeing the younger women and she shivered in fear and revulsion. Making a mental note, she vowed to speak to the ladies before she left the pub. They needed, and deserved, to be warned.

And damn him! Now she was going to have to pay for his meal! That was exactly what she was trying to get out of doing!

Or maybe he'd mooch off of one of the other villagers. No, that wasn't good, she thought. She knew everyone's financial status and none of them had money to spare. Damn him!

With a sigh, she scooted to the edge of the bench. "I'll be right back," she whispered to Callum, then walked over to the bar. "Make sure that me father's meal goes on my tab, eh?"

Arthur pulled back, glanced around the room, and smiled kindly at Fiona. "Aye, darlin'," he replied with a jerk of his head. "That's verra good of ye."

Fiona didn't bother to reply. Instead, she headed back to the table and picked up the empty bowls of stew. "I have to go," she told Callum, even though a small part of her, well, a big part of her, would love to stay and interrogate the man further. He had a hidden agenda. She could sense it, but she wasn't sure how to get the truth out of him.

Truth. It was such an odd concept for so many people.

Turning, she headed for the door, but paused and turned back to Arthur. "Please tell Sorcha tha' the stew was excellent! Better than ever!"

Arthur smiled, a flush staining his ruddy cheeks but he nodded. "Thank ye, Fi. Ye're a good woman!" He glanced over her shoulder.

"And ay like the new guy much better than that Bernard fella that's been sniffin' around ye lately."

Fiona turned and looked at Callum who was now standing near the door, obviously waiting for her. Ignoring the leap of her heart, she turned back to Arthur. "He's not..." she started to say, then stopped herself. If the villagers thought that she was dating Callum, then perhaps word might get back to Bernard and he'd stopped bothering her. "Aye. He's a good one."

Then she sauntered away, hoping that the others in the pub would also note her departure with another man and spread the news to Bernard, who really had become quite an annoyance lately.

"Ready to go?" Callum asked, pulling the door open for her. He followed her out into the chilly, night air. It was loud inside the pub, the walls more than a foot thick and made of heavy stone held in place by the thick, sticky lime-based mortar. That kind of construction kept the noise inside the pub instead of letting the sounds seep out, like the newer construction.

The darkness enveloped them, forming a cocoon of silence as they walked through the pub's parking lot. Callum slid his hands into his pants pockets to remind himself to keep his hands away from her. That confusing protective instinct reared its odd head again. He wasn't sure what had just happened in the pub between Fiona and her father, not to mention he wanted to know who this mysterious "Bernard" was. The mysteries abounded.

Why had her father come home unexpectedly? Why was Fiona eating alone at the pub instead of with her father at the castle? Was there tension in their relationship? And if so, what had caused that tension? If there was tension, could he use Fiona to help him extract revenge on her father?

No. That might have been a viable option before. But now...no. He couldn't use her. He suspected that she had been used enough. She didn't need another person using her for their own personal gain.

His brain was going a mile a minute, but his body was completely focused on the woman by his side.

"Well, this is where I turn off," she said, breaking the not-entirely-comfortable silence between them.

Callum almost chuckled as he looked down at her. "I'll walk ye home, Fi," he replied, using the nickname he'd heard the bartender use. "Fi" was so much better and more appropriate than "Fiona" he thought. Fi was lighter, more fairy-like. Fiona was so formal and stiff.

She pulled her sweater closed, crossing her arms over her stomach.

“There’s no need.” She glanced around at the dark street. “We’re pretty crime free in this village.” She turned and started walking up the hill towards the castle

Callum ignored her and continued by her side as they walked up the cobbled street lined with stone fencing. The fences kept the sheep contained and, since there were more sheep that humans in Scotland, keeping them contained was a full time job.

“Still, I’ll walk ye home.”

“Ye’re coming back to ye’re roots, Mr. MacGreggor.”

“What do ye mean?” he asked, glancing curiously down at her. She was such a tiny thing! And yet, she wasn’t. Her personality sparkled, even in the darkness. There wasn’t a moon overhead, so what was the light bouncing off her strawberry blond curls?

She offered him a brief smile, then returned her gaze to the road. “Ay can her ye’re brogue coming through a bit more now than earlier today.”

“Ah!” He had no response to that.

“Why did ye leave Scotland?”

He hesitated for a moment, then replied honestly. “Because my father lost the castle. We were kicked off the land.”

He hadn’t meant to speak so harshly, but the bitterness and anger seeped through in his words.

She stopped again, looking up at him. “What do ye mean?”

Callum stared down at her. He wanted to tell her the truth, but would that ruin his plans?

“It’s an old story,” he finally replied, then turned to start walking again. He stopped when she put a hand to his arm. Looking down, he stared at her fingers resting against his arm, fascinated by the contrast. He’d pulled on a thick, wool sweater earlier today, and her fingers were small, the skin pale against the dark blue sleeve.

Slowly, he lifted his eyes to look into her hazel gaze. He couldn’t actually see the color of her eyes because of the darkness, but his mind remembered. Callum doubted that there was anything about this woman that he wouldn’t remember long after he’d left this place.

“We have a long walk,” she prompted.

He looked up, but in the darkness, all he could see was the stone wall from the distant light coming from the pub. “Let’s go,” he urged, putting a hand to the small of her back.

And because it felt too good, he didn’t take his hand away. Nor did she move so that his hand fell off, silently telling him that she liked the contact as well.

“Will ye tell me why ye hate stew so much that it causes eh physical reaction?"

"Nope." No way in hell was he going to think back to those times. The streets were a cruel place for a teenage boy to live. Especially one as big as he was...is. Food had always been a priority in his life back then. Sometimes, food was even more desperate than personal safety.

They walked a bit further along the road in silence, then she asked, "Will ye tell me why ye keep so much of ye'reself private?"

He glanced down at her. "Are ye going to tell me why ye hate ye're father so much?"

She paused, turning to face him. For a long moment, he thought she wasn't going to answer. But then she admitted, "Because he let me mother die." Then she was walking again, leaving him behind, stunned and...stunned!

Picking up his pace, he caught up with her. "Care to elaborate?"

She glanced up at him. "Tell me why ye hate stew so much."

For several moments, Callum debated. In the end, he was too curious. "Because after my parents died, I lived on the street, sleeping in a warehouse for shelter and working whatever jobs someone would pay me to do. The only food ah could afford was canned stuff at the time. And canned beef stew was the healthiest and most filling canned food. Ah was always hungry, always scouring for food. Sometimes stealing cans was me only source of food when I couldn't afford to buy anything." He paused for a moment, obviously reliving some painful memory. Then he said, "The taste and smell of any sort of stew brings back the painful memories of that time in me life."

Holy hell! He hadn't meant to tell her all of that. A simple, "Bad can of beef stew" would have sufficed as an explanation. So, why had he admitted the real truth?

She stopped, staring up at him and he could feel the sympathy in her gaze even if he couldn't see her any longer.

"Ah'm so sorry, Callum," she whispered. "How did they die?"

"A car crash."

"That must ha' been devastating."

"Tell me," he demanded, the wash of memories making his body ache, so he changed the subject.

She turned and pressed her softness against his chest, her arms wrapping around his waist as she pressed her cheek to his heart. For a long moment, he couldn't move, couldn't accept her comfort. He started to push her away, but his hands only made it to her upper arms before she tightened her grip around him. "Ah'm so sorry that ye're parents died, leaving ye alone in the world!" she whispered and he suspected that she was close to tears.

So instead of pushing her away, rejecting her comfort, he felt his arms wrap around her slender shoulders, pulling her in. His head lowered and he felt the softness of her hair against his cheek.

They stood like that for a long moment, neither willing to move. Callum wasn't even sure if he was breathing. Prior to this moment, there were only four other people in this world who knew the truth about his parents. If anyone on his staff dared to ask about his past, they were met with a cold, impenetrable glare.

What the hell was it about Fiona? He'd never bared his soul to another human being like that!

She was a witch. That was the only reasonable explanation. He tightened his arms again and felt her snuggle closer, her nose pressing against the wool of his sweater. For a brief moment, he considered ripping the wool away so that he could feel her skin against his own, to know the sensation of her touch without any obstacles.

But they were standing in the street, in a dark area of the world, where everything he'd thought he knew was now off balance.

She pulled away, tilting her head back to stare up at him. "Thank you for that," she whispered.

Then she stepped away, leaving him cold. Cold and alone. Damn her! She couldn't offer her comfort like that and then rip it away! That wasn't fair!

She started walking again and he followed, his hands fisting at his sides in an effort to keep from pulling her back into his arms.

"Ah believe ye owe me the truth now as well." Even he could hear his brogue coming back now. It was odd, he thought. Callum hadn't realized how much effort it took to eliminate the accent from his words until he didn't need to guard his tone any longer.

He heard her sigh and wondered about that. He also wondered about the look she'd given him right before they'd departed from the pub. And he wondered how long it would take to get her back in his arms. Callum didn't doubt there would be another time when she was in his arms. And next time, he vowed that there wouldn't be any clothing to hinder his enjoyment!

"Fi," he prompted gently, instinctively knowing that whatever she was going to tell him next would be just as painful for her.

She sighed, stopped in the middle of the road and dropped her head. A moment later, she lifted her eyes and gazed up at the stars. He could feel the pain dripping from her tone as she said, "Me father wouldna let me mother see a doctor. He mocked her when she told him she was in pain." He heard the quiver in her voice. Then there was a long silence while she fought the demons from her past. Callum thought that would be the end of the explanation, but she continued. "He knew that something was wrong with her. She was such a beautiful, gentle person and the whole time, he *knew*!"

Callum started to reach for her, ready to offer her the same comfort that she'd offered to him moments before. But she continued up the street, her stride angry now.

Callum followed, not sure what to do.

"He knew that she was in pain!" she hissed, obviously realizing that he was right beside her. "He wiped her tears, an' told her that she should be strong, that the pain would pass!" She raged in the darkness. "He knew and he teased her. He mocked her. When she finally put her foot down and told him that she was going to see a doctor, it was too late. It was stage four breast cancer. The doctors said tha' the cancer had metastasized inteh her bones and invaded her lungs, which was why she had so much trouble breathing."

Callum didn't wait. He pulled her into his arms and held her close, his arms tight around her as he whispered, "Ah'm sorry," into her ear. "Ah'm so sorry!"

He felt her trembling and tightened his arms around her. She wasn't crying but he wished she would. He wished he could take the pain from her. He was tough. He could shoulder this burden for her.

Too soon, she pulled away and sniffed. "Thank ye fer that," she whispered. "Ah've never been able to tell anyone about how she'd died. Everyone around town only heard my father's story."

"Which was?"

She turned and, once again, headed for the castle. It was only a short distance away now and he knew that he wasn't done talking to her. Hell, he suspected he'd *never* be done talking with her! That witchiness made him want to hold her and talk with her and...a hell of a lot of other things...with her.

"He said tha' the cancer spread too fast fer the doctors te stop it. And if she'd only been stronger, she might ha' beaten the cancer." She laughed, the sound coming out harsh and defeated in the darkness. "He convinced everyone in the village that he was my mother's savior. But in reality, he killed her."

"Ye're father is a monumental bastard, Fi," he grumbled.

She laughed and this time, the sound was lighter. There was a tinge of happiness. "Ye're right."

"So why do ye keep him around?"

She sighed and looked into the darkness. The lights of the castle were now visible. Because of this place," she whispered. "Because ah canna imagine living anywhere other than MacGreggor Castle. It has roots and depth. There are so many problems, but the stones feel alive to me. And it seems as if the castle, or maybe the ghosts within it, are calling to me, begging me to save the building."

"I get that," he told her. "It's an ancient building with loads of history. Dozens of generations grew up there." He stared at the tall, stone edifice that was his ultimate goal. "Ah'm going to buy this place back, Fi," he warned her.

She laughed, shaking her head. "No' a chance. This is me home. If anyone is gonna to wrest control from me father's clutches, it will be me." She smiled into the darkness and, because they were closer to the castle, he could just make out her expression. "This is me home, Callum. I know that ye lived here too, but ah've rebuilt so many o' the rooms. Ah've put so much energy inteh the garden." She turned and looked up at him. "It's mine." She grimaced. "Or rather...it *will* be, once ah can somehow convince me father te sell it te me."

"How are ye going aboot doing that?"

She moved over to a stone bench and looked up at the night sky. Because the clouds had moved in over the past few hours, there wasn't a lot to see. But it was still peaceful here. Silent, but in a comforting way.

He took the seat next to her, his arm wrapping around her shoulders. He could feel the softness of her curls on his arm and wanted to let his fingers dive into the tresses, feel her against him. But he held back.

"Ah havna figured that oot yet. Years ago, ah asked him te sell the castle te me. He laughed in me face. He told me that I couldna afford his price." She closed her eyes and opened them again. "Then I hired an agent to approach my father with an anonymous offer. We made a bit of progress, but ah think me father figured oot it was me behind the offer and withdrew."

"Why is he so adamant on not selling to ye? Doesna he spend most of his time in London?"

"He does." She cringed and peeked up at him through her lashes, then quickly away. "Ah'm afraid that ah'm the reason that he won't sell te me. Ah'm me own worst enemy, so te speak."

"How so?"

Her fingers laced together tightly. "Ah canna stand having him around. So Ah bought a London flat and allow him te live there." She shook her head, causing the hair to tickle his forearm. "Ah also pay him an 'allowance' o' sorts while he pretends te ferrets out good investment opportunities." She chuckled. "At least, that's the arrangement we've had going for a while. At first, he was pretty good at it. But lately, he's been...no' so good."

"Not finding many good opportunities?"

"He's brought me several scams. Nothing legitimate. Ah think he's gotten in with a partner and they are trying te steal me blind." She chuckled softly. "What he doesna understand is that ah have several good resources to investigate the companies he suggests. Ah'm no' an idiot." She sighed and looked up at him. "Ah'm a wealthy wooman, Callum. If ye're here te try te swindle me, then ye're in fer a big surprise. Ah'm well off, but ah'm no' daft."

He smiled, and because he couldn't resist, his hand moved to stroke her hair. "Ah know ye're no' an idiot, Fi. Ye're clearly smart and savvy te boot." His eyes traveled over her features. "No' te mention, beautiful."

He gave up the internal fight. Leaning forward, he let his lips brush hers. Softly at first, but when she didn't pull back, he deepened the kiss. Her lips trembled under his, one hand coming up to singe the skin on his cheek.

Pulling her closer, he lifted her onto his lap and covered her mouth with his own, one hand on the back of her head holding her still. She did the same, grabbing his head and shifting so that she was straddling his hips. It was stunningly erotic and he briefly entertained the thought of lifting her skirts and sliding into her heat.

Unfortunately, her enthusiastic response might be hot, but it also proved that she was unskilled in the art of kissing. That translated into "not very experienced" in the sexual arena as well.

Grabbing her hips, he pulled her closer, shifting their bodies so that she was more perfectly aligned with his erection. Absorbing her gasp, he deepened the kiss even further, kissing her hard, his tongue mating with hers as he felt her roll her hips against his hardness. With one hand still on the back of her head and his other hand guiding her hips, he showed her how to ride him.

She was a quick study. Maybe, too quick! She took over, going faster and hotter, grinding against him in ways that she enjoyed, driving him wild with lust. Every shift against him with that hot, encased heat was like a stab of lust to his gut. He was in pain, but there wasn't a chance in hell that he was going to stop her. He could feel the tension increasing in her body, felt the way she moved. Then she pulled away, her mouth no longer on his. Instead, she stared down at him, her body moving faster and harder. He heard her breath catch in the back of her throat and she threw her head back...!

Her cry of delight, of release and pleasure, drifted through the night air. Thankfully, only the whispers of ghosts were around to hear her pleasure. The ghosts and Callum, he corrected, holding her steady as she collapsed against him, protecting her as she slowly recovered from her beautiful climax.

For a long time, neither of them moved. He could feel her soft, sweet breath against his neck, felt her body trembling with aftershocks, then nothing. She was silent. He wondered if she'd fallen asleep and silently vowed to protect her for as long as she needed.

But then she lifted her head and looked at him. Since she was still straddling his lap, their faces were almost level. He couldn't see her blush, but knew that's where her mind had gone.

"Ah should..." she said, awkwardly climbing off his lap. She stood beside the bench for a moment, her hands fluttering over her skirt to push everything back in order.

"Fi, stop!"

"Ah need te go inside." She hurried up the pathway to the gate for the castle, without looking back.

"Fi!" he called out, angry now, but also in too much pain to go after her.

"Tomorrow!" she called out over her shoulder as she ran into the castle. The heavy, oak door slammed with a resounding thud and she was gone.

Callum stared at the door, seriously contemplating breaking the damn door down.

No, that wouldn't be a good idea. She was embarrassed by what had happened. Fi needed some time to process what they'd just experienced together. Tomorrow, he'd stop by the castle and explain that they were two consenting adults with needs and there was nothing wrong with what had happened between them.

Turning, he headed back into the village where he'd parked his car. It was a short drive to the house he'd rented for this...incursion or whatever he was calling it now. He had more information, more reason to hate Duncan Reid, so an "incursion" didn't seem to fit any longer. But he was still so turned on from Fiona's...climax...that he couldn't think properly. Walking up the stairs, he stripped off his clothes along the way to his bedroom, unconcerned with where the clothes landed. All he knew was that he needed a cold shower.

"Damn it!" Ripping off his balaclava, the man furiously tossed it across the room. Who the hell was the huge guy walking Fiona home? She always returned to the castle alone!

It took him several minutes of pacing before he calmed down enough to think. He had to get rid of that woman! Or at least scare her off! She was tough, but he'd come up with a plan. Unfortunately, that plan didn't include some ridiculous behemoth walking her home! No way could he attack the woman with a man that size around!

Stopping in front of the rather lumpy wooden bed, he contemplated his options. Okay, he thought, getting rid of her during a nighttime walk clearly wasn't going to work. It had been a perfect plan. No witnesses, a moonless night, and a sleepy village where crime was practically unheard of. It would shock the village if they found their favorite little saint gone, but no one would have suspected him. He'd tried to get her out of the castle so he could search the nooks and crannies. But the damn woman never left! She worked upstairs in one of the bedrooms that she'd converted into an office, and the rest of the time, she was working in her garden! She occasionally went to the local grocery store, but that wasn't long enough for him to properly search the castle.

Hence, his plan to get her permanently out of the picture. He figured that, with her gone, her ass of a father would return to London and he'd have all the time in the world to find the knife. If that knife ever turned up, then his fingerprints along with the blood...he'd be convicted of murder and there'd be no way he could wiggle out of that conviction!

Gripping the footboard, he stared thoughtfully out into the dark night. He needed a new plan. Something that would work quickly. He didn't have much time. If he was recognized, then...no! He'd done a good job of changing his appearance. Now, he just needed to find that incriminating knife and he could be on his merry way!

Headlights flashed through the window, then quickly disappeared as the vehicle rounded the corner.

The lights...blind corners and sharp cliffs?

Yes! That was it! There were several wonderful roads in this village where a car could just...fall off the side of the hill! Craggy rocks and gravity would do the rest.

He clapped his hands together, the sound loud in the silence of the ancient room. Everything in this damn village was ancient. Every house was made of stone, with tiny windows and low ceilings. He hated it! Hated the uncomfortable clothes he had to wear all the time and the ridiculously tiny houses where he had to stop by for tea, act like he enjoyed the company of these irritating townspeople. He hated the irritating way he had to smile at everyone all the time...he felt like a complete nitwit! But everyone smiled around here. It was nauseating how friendly every damn villager was!

However, their friendliness, their blind belief that everyone was good, kind, and blah, blah, blah was the only reason he'd been able to slip into this persona and get so close to the villagers. They all loved him. The villagers thought he was the best thing since sliced bread!

He laughed, shaking his head at their gullible natures.

He focused on thinking through the details. He'd need access to her car. Yes, he'd make sure that her stupid, sensible car had a few engine problems! That would take care of her.

Once Fiona was out of the way, he would have free reign of the castle!

Chapter 3

Fiona stepped out of her sedan and gazed up at the lovely house. She'd known that this house existed, but she'd never been inside of it. The owners, a couple that had moved into a retirement community down in Edinburgh, rented their house out to summer travelers for additional income.

Now, standing in front of the gate, she was impressed with the beauty of the house. It was in the Tudor style, with small windows and a thatched roof, which wasn't as common in this part of Scotland. The beautiful garden was surrounded by a stone wall, which definitely *was* common in these parts.

Surveying the flowers and trees, she made note of the varieties, wondering if she could find some of them for her own garden.

Then she realized that she was procrastinating by standing here cataloguing the plants, putting off the moment when she had to face Callum again.

Breathing in slowly, she blew the air out in a whoosh. "Dunna be a coward, Fi!" she reprimanded herself.

Hearing the words, she straightened her spine, pulled her shoulders back, and forced her feet to carry her forward. Lifting her hand to knock on the door was one of the most difficult things she'd had to do in a long time.

The knock sounded extraordinarily loud in the silence of the morning. Turning, she lifted her face up to the sunshine, hoping the extra warmth would give her a bit of courage.

Callum stepped out of the shower and grabbed a towel, wondering how he could "accidentally" run into Fiona this morning. He thought he'd heard a knock on the front door and stilled. But when he didn't hear anything else, he wrapped the towel around his waist and headed barefoot into the surprisingly large bedroom.

The rental house came with daily maid service, but Callum had declined that luxury, wanting more privacy for this particular mission. At home, he was usually out of his house before his housekeeper showed up each morning. Working eighteen or twenty hour days didn't allow for a lot of time to clean one's house, so a housekeeper was necessary.

No, this was a personal mission.

Another knock sounded and he swiveled around, listening. That was definitely a knock and it was coming from the front door.

Peering out the front window, he spotted a very sensible sedan outside. The vehicle was probably ten years old, maybe older, but well maintained.

Fiona!

He grabbed a pair of jeans and hurried down the stairs. He didn't bother with a shirt.

Yanking open the front door, he stared down at the lovely woman, startled all over again by how pale her skin was, her dark, hazel eyes contrasting with the strawberry blond curls framing her dainty features.

His woman! Yes, after last night, he'd begun to think of her as his woman. The whole walk home, he'd considered ways to get her to understand what he innately grasped. They were meant to be together. She was his woman and he was her man. There was an attraction between them that was intense and unavoidable.

Laying in the enormous bed upstairs last night, he'd made a plan. Oh, he wasn't abandoning his revenge towards Duncan Reid. No, that was a given. The man had to be destroyed. Hearing Fiona explain about her mother last night had merely reinforced his need to make the man suffer.

Standing in front of Fiona now, all of his plans came rushing back. Not that they'd ever really left. Hell, he'd been thinking about her or dreaming about her ever since last night.

Now he knew that she was even more beautiful than he'd remembered. The morning sunshine was a soft kiss against her skin, a shimmering glitter in her hair. She was...hell, when had he become a freaking poet?

"Ye're here." Silently, Callum berated himself for stating the obvious.

Reaching out, he grabbed her wrist and gently pulled her into the house, then slammed the door closed. When they were finally alone, away from the prying eyes of whoever might be passing by, he leaned in closer, bracing a hand above her head as he inhaled her sweet, feminine fragrance. "What can I do for ye, Fi?" he asked, his voice huskier than he intended. He was trying to hide his need for her, but obviously not doing a very good job.

"I...um..." her eyes flicked down to his mouth, then back to his eyes. It was a brief moment, but he caught it and knew that she wanted him to kiss her. "Ah wanted to discuss something with ye."

Callum didn't move. "Ah'm listening."

"Could we...?" Fiona tried to glance around him, but she couldn't see much. Not with those broad shoulders of his blocking her view.

"Aye," he replied, moving closer. "Anything ye want, Fi," he promised.

Licking her lips, she wondered if he was thinking what she was thinking. Probably, but maybe not in the same way.

"Ye're scaring me, Callum," she whispered.

Immediately, he pushed away from the wall and even took a step back. His enormous, bare arms crossed over an equally bare chest, emphasizing the muscles in those arms.

"Why are ye here?"

She blinked, startled by his directness. Her plan had been so easy in the privacy of her own bedroom. It had seemed reasonable and even manageable.

But she hadn't been face to chest with the real man. She hadn't remembered how big and intimidating he was.

"Ah have a proposition fer ye." She looked around. "But ah was hoping tha' we might have some tea and talk?"

"Of course," he replied, already heading for a doorway. She followed, desperately wishing that she had another reason for being here. Of course, her real reason was a good one. It just seemed so...mercenary now.

Stepping into the cheerful, yellow kitchen, she looked around instead of staring at the man's bare back with the fascinating, rippling muscles as Callum dumped coffee grounds into a coffee maker. "Is coffee okay? It's all Ah have at the moment."

"Ay, of course. Tha's fine. Wonderful, actually." She paused for a brief moment, then continued nervously in an effort to fill the silence. "Ah usually have coffee in the morning, then switch te herbal tea in the afternoon. Ah sometimes have trouble sleeping when Ah've had too much caffeine or if Ah've had coffee too late in the day."

He pressed a button on the coffee maker, then turned, leaning against the countertop as he looked across the expanse of the kitchen at her.

She glanced up at him, then quickly away, folding her hands in front of her. "Stop watching me like that."

"Like what?"

"Like ye're a starving man and ye're going te eat me." She realized what she'd just said, how it came across, moments after the words were uttered. Then she felt her cheeks flare with that embarrassing heat and cursed her pale skin. Every blush showed on her cheeks! "Ah didna mean tha' ye were...tha' ye were thinking...!"

"Ah am."

He said it so casually, it took her several moments to absorb the meaning of his words.

"Ye are?"

"Aye." He pushed away from the counter and came towards her. Predator to prey. Lion to lamb. His eyes held her still, promising pleasure as his feet carried him closer. Closer to her destruction. "All night, Ah thought about ye. About wha' I wanted te do te ye." He was mere inches from her now as he continued. "And aye, Ah want te know what ye taste like. Ah want te know wha' ye sound like when ye climax against me tongue."

"Dear heaven!" she whispered, surprised that she still had the capacity to speak.

"Does tha' mean tha' ye want me too?"

His hands were down by his sides, not touching her. But oh, it would be so nice if he would just reach out and touch her, send those delicious shivers through her body, remind her of why she'd come here. Why she'd stupidly put herself in a position where she would feel this awkward and embarrassed.

"Aye."

Where in the world had she come up with the courage to say that?

His eyes flared but he didn't move. "Is tha' why ye came over here this morning?"

Was it? Yes. No! Okay, all of the above.

She cleared her throat and lifted her chin. "Ah came here te make a deal with ye."

The lifting of his dark eyebrow warned her that he wasn't of a mind to make deals. Make love? Yeah, he was all over that!

Fiona stepped away from the man, needing distance and fresh air. Breathing in the clean, male scent of him was distracting. She couldn't think when he was so close.

Turning, she placed her hands on the butcher block island, pulled in a slow, deep breath, then let it out before she looked up at him.

"Ah didna come here te discuss having an affair with ye."

"Pity," he replied, crossing those magnificent arms over his chest. Images of those arms wrapped around her, his hands caressing her, that mouth...!

She blinked and shook her head, forcing her gaze toward her hands. The wood. The butcher block. Anywhere but at his muscular chest with the light sprinkling of hair and those flat nipples that she'd love to...!

Stop it! Another breath, then her eyes flew open as she heard a chuckle. A deep, masculine chuckle that sent warning flares of desire straight down her spine to pool, sizzling, low in her belly.

"Cream or sugar?" he asked.

Fiona looked up in time to watch those back muscles ripple as he reached for two mugs. Cream or sugar? She'd love both. All over him so that she could...!

"Stop it!" she hissed.

Callum glanced back over his shoulder with a dark, raised eyebrow. "No coffee?"

She bit her lip for a moment, then shook her head. "Nay. Ah mean," she groaned, hiding her face in her hands. "Would ye *please* put a shirt on?"

Another chuckle, then fingers wrapped around her wrists, pulling her hands away. He then kissed her forehead. "Aye. Ah'll go put a shirt on since me chest is clearly bothering ye." He kissed her cheek, sensuously close to her ear, making her shiver. "Once Ah'm fully dressed, I'd like te hear what ye came te talk aboot. But after that conversation, Ah'd like te talk about a few *other* things. Will ye agree?"

"Te talking?" she asked, needing clarification.

"Aye. Just talking," he confirmed. "Fer now."

Fiona stared into Callum's eyes, trying to slow her heartrate. But that was impossible when she could feel the warmth of his hands on her waist and his scent, that damn scent of him kept invading her nostrils.

Still, she needed his help. Her efforts towards her ultimate goal so far had failed and Callum might have the key to her eventual success.

"Fine. Talk. Aye." She stepped back, relieved when his hands dropped from her waist. "After ye put on a shirt."

Callum laughed softly as he headed for the door. "I take my coffee black, but there's milk in the fridge and sugar on the shelf. Help ye'rself. Ah'll be right back."

Fiona breathed a sigh of relief when he finally left the room. Leaning heavily against the wooden countertop, she briefly rested her head in her hands. "Pull yerself together! This isna who ye are!"

"Then...who are ye?"

Fiona jerked upright in time to see Callum return, pulling on a light blue dress shirt . He hadn't buttoned it yet, so that amazing chest was still visible. His arms and shoulders were hidden, so she was only ninety-five percent distracted. A start, anyway.

He came closer, pinning her against the countertop as he placed his hands on the wood behind her.

One dark eyebrow lifted in question and she tried valiantly to remember what he'd asked her. Who was she? At this moment, she had no clue. Men had never affected her the way Callum did. Men were nice. Sometimes they caught her eye briefly as they walked down the street, but she'd never stared at a man for more than a moment before returning to whatever she'd been doing.

So this...this fascination with his naked body and his scent and his arms and...well, everything...it wasn't her! It wasn't normal.

Lifting her eyes higher, she looked into his dark eyes. "Ah'm an excellent mathematician and Ah've used me skills te figure out which stocks or companies will increase in value," she told him. Her chin went up. "Ah'm also extremely good at helping businesses thrive. Ah've worked hard with the people in this village, explaining te them how they can increase their revenues and profits, sell their products online, streamline their supply issues, and grow their businesses." She grabbed one of his wrists and, ignoring the strength under her fingers, moved his hand from behind her and reached for the coffee pot. She grabbed two mugs as she continued. "What Ah havena been successful at is getting me father te sell me the castle and estate." She turned, handing him a mug. "Ah've lived in that castle fer most of me life. As soon as Ah returned from university and started making money, Ah began rebuilding the castle. It's an extraordinarily expensive home, bu' Ah love every stone in tha' building. There used to be leaks in the walls and roof, creating mold and damaging the mortar. It used to be cold and difficult te live in. The plumbing has been updated and the electrical wiring is new. I cook and bake in the renovated kitchen and," she paused, briefly closing her eyes, then opened them to look him in the eye. "And I've built up the gardens, bringing them back to their previous glory. I know that gardens in ancient times wouldna ha' been a priority except for the herbs, but Ah think that the current gardens enhance the beauty o' the castle."

"I agree," he replied, and she tried very hard to ignore the spark of happiness that his words engendered inside of her.

"Thank ye," she whispered, then rallied. "Ah want me home. I've made several offers to me father, both personally and through various agents. Bu' he willna sell." She wrapped her fingers around the hot mug, trying to gain strength from that heat. "It's my fault tha' he willna sell. He's using me. Ah know he is."

"How is he using ye?" he asked.

She looked up at him. He knew, she thought. She could see the knowledge in his eyes and her shame increased. "Because Ah pay him te live in London," she admitted. "Ah bought a London flat and he lives there until he runs out of money. Then he comes back te the castle, te the place that I've spend too many hours and so much money fixing te turn it into a real home. He comes back and invades my world." Her chin trembled and she closed her eyes, refusing to cry. Not again!

"He killed my mother. But Ah wilna let him take me home from me." She opened her eyes again, wiping angrily at the tears. She took a deep breath and let it out, straightened her shoulders. "I suspect tha' ye've come here fer revenge. Ya want me father te pay for what he did te yer parents. Ye think he swindled yer father out o' ownership o' the castle." She didn't wait for confirmation but nodded. "Ah think you're right, but I canna prove it. And even if Ah could, that would mean that ownership of the castle would revert te ye and I canna let that happen. That castle is mine!"

"Fiona," he started to say, even stepping closer, but she put a hand up, stopping him.

"Nay, let me finish." She paused and pulled herself together again. "I dinna know ye well enough yet, but Ah suspect that ye dinna *really* want ownership o' the castle. Ye just want revenge on me father." Her chin jutted upwards again. "I propose tha' we work together. Ah have the money te buy back the castle from me father. But Ah doubt ye want that. It would give me father a large amount of money, which would make him happy." She shrugged lightly. "He'd spend it quickly, assuming Ah'd pay his living expenses again." She shook her head, unaware of how the overhead lights sparkled off of her strawberry blond curls. "But I wouldna. Our aims arenna exactly the same, bu' they are connected."

Callum stared down at her, not sure how to respond. She thought he didn't want ownership of the castle? How could she think that? It was his heritage! The castle had been in his family for generations! It was his birthright!

And yet, he could see her point as well. He remembered the castle being a dark, dank place to live. His father had kept up the maintenance on the various living quarters as well as he could, but the rest of the castle had been a crumbling mess. He hadn't bothered with the exterior either. Castles were built for strength and to intimidate one's enemies, to protect the villagers if anyone dared to attack. No one ever bothered to make the castle beautiful. Centuries ago, there would have been a kitchen garden, a space that would provide nourishment to the castle residents with herbs and vegetables. But the actual building was a bulwark against invasion. Not a thing of beauty.

Fiona had changed that. He could see the castle in his head as it was now. Not as it had been during his youth. And it was lovely. She'd done a great deal to fix it, to make it a home.

She huffed a bit, shifting on her feet impatiently. "Look, ye're an extremely wealthy man." She paused, waiting for him to deny it. He didn't. "No amount of money is going to convince me father to sell the castle. I thought I could just keep raising the offer amount and eventually, I'd reach a point when he'd be too greedy to turn the offer down."

"But the castle represents something else te ye're father, aye?"

She nodded. "Aye. Ah've finally figured out there are two things me father loves about that building."

"That ye'll continue te pay his living expenses in London as long as he owns the castle?"

She lowered her head, nodding. "Ay. That's a pretty big issue. And Ah'm ashamed that Ah have been so easily manipulated. I kept telling myself that, if I didna keep him happy and pay his expenses, then he'd get fed up and sell the castle te someone else, someone who would want it just as badly as I do. That would mean Ah'd have te leave." She sighed. "Ah've been a coward."

"What's the other issue?"

She pressed her lips together before she said, "Me father thinks o' himself as an aristocrat. The previous owners of that castle were all earls. They were genuinely Scottish aristocracy." She nodded to him. "Ye now hold tha' title, I understand."

He shrugged, dismissing her comment. "That's true. But I don't use the title. Ever."

She smiled, shaking her head. "Ye Americans never really cared much for the nobility, did ye?"

He shrugged. "We still have an elite class who manipulate the economic systems in order te maintain their status. But they dinna hold actual titles."

"And some people are smart enough te break through those controls." She tilted her head towards him. "Ye are one o' those people. Ye're one o' the wealthiest men in the United States."

He shrugged, neither confirming nor denying her statement. "So, what are ye proposing?"

She smiled. "Ah'm amazed at your modesty. Most men would ha' stated their net worth in an effort te impress me."

He chuckled. "Fi, are you seriously going te tell me you're not one o' the wealthiest women in Europe?"

She blushed and shook her head. "Ah dinna know, nor do I care. Ah've accumulated wealth because I can see the mathematical trends in various industries and Ah enjoy the mental challenges o' those trends."

"And that's not enough?"

Her glare intensified. "Ah don't care about money, Callum. Nor do ye, if I'm reading ye correctly." She paused, and again, he didn't deny it. "Ah want me home. I want ownership o' the castle and I want my father locked oot so he canna get inside an' steal from me."

"Ye consider the money you give him te be theft?"

She laughed, but there wasn't any amusement in the sound. "Nay. I mean, he *literally* steals from me. He was looking at a box yesterday with what he probably thinks is a big emerald on the outside. It's no' even glass. It's just a piece o' plastic that Ah bought at the craft store and glued onto a box that I spray painted metallic gold." She grinned and this time, her eyes sparkled. "Ah've found that putting oot cheap replicas irritates him. I've stopped buying anything o' real value because he just steals it and sells it. Obviously, the amount of money Ah pay him isna enough, since he still steals things every time he visits."

"He sounds like a real piece of..." Callum started to say one thing, but ended with, "slime."

She nodded curtly. "Tha' he is. But putting a label on the man and calling him names doesna help me...*our*...cause. What's ye're plan?"

He took a slow sip of coffee, organizing his thoughts before answering. "My original plan isna going to work."

"Why not?"

"Because ye're the source o' his income." He frowned thoughtfully. "Ah was going te convince ye te stop financing his lifestyle."

She groaned. "Tha' can be done. But he'll just find someone else te mooch off o'. I sort of felt like I was performing a public service by keeping him funded."

He grinned. "One problem at a time."

Fiona looked at him carefully, noting the gleam in his eyes. "Ye already have a plan."

His smile widened. "O' course I do."

"Care te share?"

He moved closer to her. "Ye came here te strike a bargain with me?"

"Aye," she replied.

For a brief moment, she considered just walking away from the castle, finding a new place to make her own. Maybe if she moved out and let her father maintain ownership of the castle, then she could find some happiness. Her gaze moved over Callum's chest. Happiness and perhaps a relationship?

No, she couldn't leave the castle in the hands of her father. He wouldn't care for the castle. He wouldn't continue the needed renovations or the constant maintenance that even she sometimes considered a burden.

The castle was her home. It was her sanctuary from the world. She'd rescued that building. She'd built it up and restored it to its former glory. There was no way she was going to just step back and let her father, the careless, cruel, insensitive jerk, have control of something she'd revived.

Living in a small village and making her life among the residents, she'd accepted that she would be single and childless. She'd channeled her mothering needs into that garden and into the house.

So this was her chance.

"Ay, I want te team up with ye. I have some ideas, but what do ye have in mind?"

Callum grinned as relief flooded through him. He'd watched the debate in her eyes, knew that she wasn't sure about his motives or even what he might suggest.

But he knew that she loved that castle, probably more than he did. For him, the castle was a symbol of revenge. It was also his heritage, but he could see that the castle was also in her blood. It was her baby.

Perhaps there was a way that they could both win what they most desired.

He let his eyes move down over her figure, his smile widening as he noticed the blush creeping up her throat. Yes, she understood that he was dangerous. But she had no idea how dangerous!

"Poker."

Startled, she blinked. "Poker? Ye mean...the card game?"

"Aye." He pushed away and picked up his cup of coffee. "Poker. The card game."

"Ye...enjoy playing poker?"

"Aye," he replied with a slow nod. "And I'm damn good a' it, too." He sipped his coffee. "Me friends are excellent. Some days, they're even better than me...but, if you *ever* tell them that Ah said that, I will deny it."

She laughed and the sound reverberated through his very bones. That sound...she didn't laugh enough. Not nearly enough! How could she? The woman lived and worked in the castle, hiding herself away behind those stone walls that she loved so dearly. He doubted she ever left the village except to occasionally travel to Edinburgh.

Definitely not enough laughter in her life.

"What will ye're friends do?"

"Play poker, o' course."

She blinked at him, still not understanding. He continued, "You mentioned that your father maintains ownership of the castle, but he doesna really care aboot it. Not like ye do."

"Right."

"He only holds onto it because, in his mind, it represents an aristocratic and elite status within the community and among his peers. Tha's something he craves?"

She was clearly still confused, but she nodded. "Aye. He grew up dirt poor and tells everyone that he clawed his way up the social and financial ladder te achieve all that he has today." She grimaced. "What he doesna tell everyone is tha' he cheats his way through life, stepping on anyone that can advance his need te be perceived as wealthy and significant."

Callum nodded. "Ah suspected as much, but tha's difficult te prove. And there's no way I can prove tha' he cheated me father out o' the castle because it was so long ago."

"But he did," she asserted firmly. "I dinna know how, but Ah'm sure me father did cheat yours."

There was a moment of silence as Callum absorbed the sudden pain from that assurance. Then he did what he'd always done since that horrible day when the police told him of his parents' death. He moved on. He forced himself to think about the present – and the future.

It was a struggle, but as the pain began to win, he felt a soft touch to his chest. His eyes popped open. He hadn't even been aware of closing them. But looking down, he saw his pain reflected in Fiona's eyes and his arms automatically wrapped around her.

"Wha' just happened, Callum?" she whispered, her hazel eyes cloudy with concern.

Shaking his head, he let his hand drift upwards, stroking her back. "Nothing important," he lied.

She sighed, and pressed her forehead to his chest, hiding her expression. "I think tha' it was painfully important. And probably had something te do with me father." She stepped away from him again, folding her arms across her chest. "Wha' can Ah do te help ye gain vengeance against me father and ownership o' me home."

"Tell me more aboot ye're father."

She tilted her head slightly, then grinned. "Ye want me te explain his 'tells' te ye."

He grinned, impressed by how quickly she grasped the situation. "Exactly."

She pondered briefly, then shook her head. "Nay. I want te know the whole plan, wha' ye'll get oot o' it and what Ah will get oot o' it." She straightened. "Me father is a cheat and a liar. He manipulates people fer a living. So, whatever ye ha' planned, I want te know wha' it is, the desired outcome, how ye see each step going, and–"

She stopped when he kissed her. Fiona was too startled to react immediately, but at the feel of his fingers diving into her hair so that he could tilt her head and deepen the kiss, she whimpered, wrapping her arms around his neck. She needed something to brace herself with because her world had just tilted dramatically!

Every argument against kissing him, this dangerous, potentially soul-drugging man, melted away. There were no consequences flitting through the back of her mind, no list of activities she needed to accomplish today.

All she knew was that he was kissing her, demanding that she open her mouth, to taste him, to truly experience a kiss with a man that set her senses on fire with just a glance.

Now she could touch him, she could feel those muscles that she'd admired this morning. Running her fingers from his shoulders to the bare skin revealed by his open shirt, Fiona reveled in the unexpected and unfamiliar desire. Her body melted into a heated liquid, her mind skittering and her body curving into him.

When he finally lifted his head, she felt... enflamed. Her nipples were tight, her breasts felt swollen, pressing against the normally adequate confines of her bra. And her core! Goodness, she'd never felt such throbbing down there! Her previous boyfriends had been nice. They'd been very kind, intelligent men. But none, never, had any of them made her body throb like this!

Shaking, she pulled her trembling fingers away and leaned against the countertop. "Tha' was...um..." she paused, pushing her hair out of her eyes, then lifted her gaze to look into his. "Why did ye kiss me?"

"Because ye are a beautiful woman tha' makes me blood burn." He took her hand and pressed her shaking fingers against his erection. "This is what you do to me, Fiona."

She pulled her hand away quickly, feeling as if she'd invaded his privacy somehow, even though he'd been the one to put her hand there! His brogue was thick and heavy, making her heart throb with pleasure!

"I dinna...!"

"Ye dinna believe tha' men could desire ye, do ye?"

"Nay!"

"Because ye've sequestered yerself back here in a sleepy village, hibernating in your office and no' going oot into the real world often enough te tempt yerself."

Her eyes flared, her chin lifting defiantly. "Ye dinna ken anything about me life, Callum. Dinna make assumptions aboot what A do or dinna do!"

"Am I wrong?"

She couldn't answer him in the negative, so she ignored the question. "The plan!" she asserted firmly. "What's ye're plan?"

He chuckled, but stepped back. "Okay, I'll slow down. For now, Fi. But soon, ye're no' going te be able te hide behind the villagers o' ye're work. We're going te explore this attraction atween us."

"The plan!" she huffed, feeling light-headed at the thought of exploring anything with Callum. He was just so...big and male! Too confident in his sexuality.

Nope, Fiona had learned to just ignore sex. It was easier that way. No disappointment if she never hoped for something she couldn't have.

So, she wasn't entirely thrilled with his assertion that they would explore this...whatever it was...that flared up whenever they were together.

However, she could no longer state that men, as a species, weren't attracted to her. The evidence of Callum's attraction was right there in front of her. That evidence was pretty difficult to ignore, and just thinking about it made her feel all soft and squishy inside.

"Could we please focus on the plan?" she begged, feeling ridiculous when she heard her pleading tone.

"Ye're no' ready." He nodded and took her hand. "I ken." He didn't release her hand, but picked up her cup of coffee and handed it to her. "Let's go ootside in the sunshine and talk."

Relieved, she nodded, cradling her still-hot coffee as she followed him out of the house. He led her to a beautiful, enclosed backyard filled with heather, primrose, and bluebells. The lush flowers were soothing, and inviting to sit beside and contemplate the world.

"This is beautiful!" she sighed, feeling better now that she was surrounded by flowers. Nature always did that for her. Any time she made a mistake, lost money on the stock market, or a business didn't come through the way she'd calculated, Fiona would go outside into her garden and her world would become right again.

Callum looked around as he sat down in the chair opposite hers. "I thought so as well. Ah was surprised te find a house like this so close to ye're village. It's far enough te be oot o' the way, but still close enough tha' I dinna feel entirely oot o' touch."

She took a sip of her coffee and tried not to stare at his shirt, which was still open. "Ye're plan?" she prompted.

He chuckled, then rested his coffee cup on his knee. "I think we should start a game o' poker with some o' the locals. Just you an' me, and we'll let the locals win most o' the pot."

She nodded. "Okay, I'm on board so far." She shook her head, batting impatiently at the curls that danced around her cheeks. "I dinna understand how that will help us, though."

"We'll only start with the locals. And letting them win most o' the money means that we'll lull Duncan into a false sense of confidence."

"Okay. Again, good so far."

"Then we'll bring in the big guns. Still playing with the locals, but we'll spread word that some pretty big names are coming inte town te play with us."

Tilting her head, she looked at him, trying to figure out his plan. "Who do you have in mind?"

He smiled crookedly. "Ha' ye ever heard of a lawyer named Angela Bertuccio?"

Fiona rolled her eyes. "Of course I have. She won tha' big lawsuit last year against the pharmaceutical company." Her eyes narrowed. "She married James Rothschild. I talk te him on a regular basis. He's an investor as well. He and I compete on some issues, but we've also collaborated on a few projects."

"Exactly," Callum replied. "Angela and James are good friends of mine."

"Nay!" she snapped, shaking her head. "No' a chance. I consider James to be a friend o' mine, and Angela Bertuccio? She's like...a legend! She's my hero! She's a role model te women who are trying te make it in the legal and business world." She shook her head again. "I'll no' let them near me father! He might contaminate them."

Callum chuckled. "Dinna underestimate me friends. We regularly play poker together. But all o' me friends are good in the business world. They know how te read people well enough te have made it after..." he paused and Fiona saw his eyes shutter, "...challenging issues in their lives."

"Challenging how?" she asked, curious. His comments were so mysterious. Learning how he'd met his friends would give her more insights into this fascinating man.

He shook his head. "The details arena important. What's relevant fer our plan te work is tha' they are excellent at reading the signs various players give off during poker games." He leaned forward, resting his elbows on his knees as he watched her intently. "But you," he paused for a moment, those dark eyes looking over her features. "I suspect that you are an expert a' reading ye're father. Am I right?"

She hesitated for only a moment. "Ah might be. What would me contribution te this enterprise be?" She saw the hesitation and shook her head. "Dinna even think aboot keeping me oot o' this game ye're planning," she admonished, amusement in her voice. "There's no way that I'm going to be left oot." She shifted, her hands folding over her knees. "Me father has manipulated me through his lies and his cheating ways ever since Ah can remember." She tilted her head. "Did I mention tha' he fought with me mum to keep me out of school, so that he could use me te lure his suckers into a false sense o' security?"

His eyes widened and Fiona nodded before continuing. "Yep. Even on the days when me mum refused to let him have his way, he'd show up at my school, tell the headmaster and my teachers that there was a death in the family and," she lowered her voice that was now dripping with sarcasm, "we had a lot o' deaths in my family in those days." Then she lifted her chin and continued. "Then he'd bring me with him te a 'business meeting' where he would regale potential investors with his illegal scams, with me standing by his side." She sighed and shook her head. "I canna tell ye how many diseases he came up with for me mother's absence and her inability te take care o' me." She pressed her lips together slightly, then continued. "So ye need me. I know how me father lies. I know when he's aboot te go in for a zinger an' when he's bluffing."

"Aye, but if ye're playing poker wi' us, then how are ye going te warn us tha' he's bluffing o' telling the truth?"

She contemplated that for a moment, then shrugged. "Me father is going te cheat."

"I'm taking tha' for granted."

"So if he's going te cheat, then how aboot if we play by his rules?"

Callum relaxed back against the cushions of the chair. "What are ye thinking?"

She smiled, her mind whirling with the possibilities. "What aboot if I sit in a secret room and watch him? Ah could relay information te ye aboot wha' he's doing."

"Ye mean sit behind him and tell us wha' cards he has in his hands?"

She chuckled, shaking her head. "Nay. He's too smart fer that." She tapped her fingers restlessly against her knee. "Besides, Ah don't like the idea o' cheating in that way." She shifted. "Nay, wha' I'm suggesting is that I sit in an area where I can observe my father's body language and his expressions. I know his tells. I know when he's lying simply by the way he tilts his head or shifts his body. Most people arna adept a' reading him because most people are used to someone with empathy and emotions." She shook her head again. "Most people think all sociopaths are serial killers. But in my father's case, he's a textbook sociopath that uses his lack of emotions te manipulate everyone 'round him. He doesna even realize he's doing it, most of the time. It's just natural for him. Because he has no emotions, he is more able to analyze other people's emotions and use them against them. Even the slightest hesitation, a moment of inhaled breath or a look to the side would give my father an advantage."

"And ye think ye can see these 'tells' an' inform the rest o' the group?"

Her smile was slow in coming, but she nodded her head. "Absolutely. I've made it me life's work to know when me father is lying."

He whistled. "Ah think that your ability te read him would be an excellent advantage while playing poker."

She grinned. "Excellent!"' She stood up and picked up her now-empty coffee cup. "Let me know when the first game is set up. I should be in on it and I'll lose to him. No' by much, because that would be too obvious." She turned and said over her shoulder. "He's no' an idiot. But nay am I."

Callum stood up as well, watching her hips sway as she walked back into the cottage. She was sexy as hell, her confidence in high gear now. She might be relatively innocent in so many areas, but when it came to her father, she was an expert.

He followed her inside, watching as she grabbed her cardigan off of the back of a chair. He hadn't even noticed her taking it off before. But she flung the soft wool over her shoulders, then glanced up at him. "How long will it take te organize?"

"A couple o' days."

She looked disappointed and Callum wondered if she was sad because they wouldn't see each other. He realized he didn't like the idea either.

"But I think we should get together tomorrow te discuss which villagers would be good te have in the first few games. The ones that are just between you, me, an' a few others. The initial games will be the enticement."

"My father wilna think that playing poker wi' the villagers, especially if I'm there, te be much incentive te pay attention."

He shook his head and pulled the front door open. "Ah dinna think so either. But it's just the opening gambit." He put his hand to the small of her back when she stepped out, walking beside her along the stone path. "I've learned that a soft opening is best when one is trying te sneak up on one's opponent."

She grinned, sliding on a pair of sunglasses. "Tha' sounds like an excellent plan." Fiona then reached into her purse to grab her car keys, turning away from the temptation Callum presented. She didn't want to leave. She kept replaying those kisses, wondering what it would be like if she stepped back into his arms and asked him to kiss her again.

But she wasn't that kind of woman. She wasn't sexually confident. The men in her past had been less than complimentary about her sexual prowess, so instead of going up onto her toes and kissing him goodbye, shooting him a 'come hither' look over her shoulder as she walked away, she pressed her lips together and hurried for her car.

"Stop!" Callum called out.

Fiona jerked to a halt and turned, eyes wide as she looked back at him.

But Callum wasn't looking at her. His gaze was directed downwards, staring at the street. When she followed his eyes, she noticed a trail of yellowish-brown liquid seeping from underneath her car and into the grass beside the driveway.

"Oh no!" she gasped, rushing closer. "What is it? Did I hit something?"

She bent down, not wanting to see if an animal was captured underneath her car, but unable to ignore the possibility that she'd hurt a living creature. There were rabbits galore in the village. She hated them, but she'd never actually harm them. Instead, she either didn't grow the plants that they preferred, or sprayed garlic spray on them regularly. The rabbits seriously hated the scent of garlic.

"It's not an animal," Callum replied, gently but forcibly pulling her back. "That's brake fluid."

She glanced up at him, startled by his words. "Brake fluid?" She didn't fully understand, then looked down the road. Not all of the roads in the village were well tended. "Did I hit a rock or something?"

He stretched out beside the car and slid beneath it. He pulled out his cell phone and turned on the flashlight app so he could properly examine the undercarriage.

Fiona watched, her hands braced on her knees. Anxiously, she waited for him to tell her what was wrong. She probably needed a new car. This one was over ten years old, but Donegan, her mechanic in the east side of the village, inspected all the parts twice a year, repairing or replacing anything that needed it. He hadn't mentioned any problems with her brakes and, if her memory was correct, he'd replaced the brake pads about eighteen months ago. It might have been two years ago, she wasn't certain. But she was sure that Donegan would have warned her the last time she'd brought the car in for maintenance if there was something wrong with the brakes.

A moment later, Callum pulled himself out from underneath the car, shaking his head as he dusted his hands together.

"What's wrong with me car?" she asked, her stomach tightening.

"Who has had access to ye're car recently?" he asked.

"No one," she replied firmly. "I park me car in the garage at the castle."

"Do ye lock the garage at night?"

She frowned at him as if he'd just said that she should travel to the moon. "Nay. Why should I? There's no crime here in the..."

"Fiona!" another male voice called out.

Fiona and Callum turned as one, watching with interest as Father Finn rushed down the street. "Father Finn?" she called back, shielding her eyes from the sunshine. "What are ye doing here?"

The priest came to a stop, bending forward and bracing his hands against his knees as he struggled to catch his breath. "I just," he gasped, still panting. When he finally caught his breath, he looked at her. "I saw someone under your car an' hurried over." He looked behind her with a glare. "What are ye doin' to the lass' car, mister?"

Callum cocked an eyebrow. "And who are you?"

The man eyed the liquid flowing along the street and looked at Callum, an easy grin spreading across his boyish features. Quickly, he stepped forward, extending his hand. "Father Avril Finnegan, at your service, me friend!" He chuckled, his smile widening. "Most people just call me Father Finn though. Easier on the tongue."

Callum glared at the man, resenting his easy manner around Fiona. He knew his reaction didn't make any sense. Surely it couldn't be jealousy. Over a priest? The man was a member of the clergy!

And yet, Callum sensed something else about him. Something that belied his priestly garments.

Again, that didn't make any sense, but he'd run into too much confusion over the past few days. Ever since coming here to the village to reclaim MacGreggor Castle, his perception of the right and wrongs he'd always thought were etched in stone, were turning out to be...less than accurate.

So perhaps being jealous of a priest wasn't so off the mark.

He shook the guy's hand, noticing that the priest's palms were sweaty. Not a good sign. It indicated that the man was nervous. About being around Fiona? Callum's gaze moved from the priest to his woman, wanting to grip the guy's hand harder to convey that he should give up any idea of something more than a religious or friendly relationship with Fi. But the man's fingers were too soft, too...oddly delicate.

"Fiona, what's going on with your car?"

Was there a slightly breathless quality to his question?

"I dinna ken," Fiona responded. "I was just about to drive home when Callum saw something was wrong." She was staring down at the still-seeping fluid, but looked up when she finished her explanation. "I guess I should call Donegan an' ask him te tow the car te his shop fer a look."

"Eh, I doubt that there's anythin' seriously wrong with the car if Donegan regularly examines it. And ye're one of the most conscientious people around. So I'm sure ye take care of ye're car, lass." He glanced over at Callum. "I'm sure she can drive it home."

"Not a chance," Callum growled. "*I'll* drive her." He turned to look at Fiona. "I'll have someone come tow the car and fix the issue."

Fiona shook her head. "No need. Donegan is a competent mechanic. Plus, he knows my car extremely well. I'll just call and ask him to take care of it."

"Fi," he replied, not saying anything more. She looked up, hesitating with her finger hovering over the cell phone.

"I can just..." she stopped when he continued looking at her. Then she closed her mouth and nodded, sliding the cell phone back into her purse. "Right. I'd appreciate ye're help."

Father Finn's gaze shifted back and forth between them, obviously confused by the unspoken conversation. But Callum ignored him.

"Well then," Father Finn said, clapping his hands together. "How aboot if I escort ye home then? I was out on a wee walk te take in the glorious sunshine, but we could walk back te the church and I could..."

"I'll drive her home," Callum reiterated firmly.

Fiona lifted her hand, but Callum was getting an odd feeling from the other man. He took Fiona's hand in his, squeezing her fingers firmly as he nodded sharply to the priest. "Dinna let us interrupt ye're walk, Father."

The man looked startled at the abrupt dismissal, hesitated, but when Callum tugged at Fiona's hand and they both turned to leave, the priest finally continued on with his walk.

"Tha' was so rude of ye," Fiona hissed moments before he tugged her through a door that led to a darkened garage.

"I dinna care," he said, spinning her around and pressing her back against the black sedan parked in the darkness. "Something is off about that priest. I canna put my finger on it, but there's something...not right."

Fiona's breath left her lungs the moment he spun her around, his heavy hands on her hips and she waited, breathlessly, for him to kiss her again. She wanted so much more, but she'd be happy with a kiss.

Invitingly, she tilted her head back, her hands resting lightly on his upper arms. "Is that so?" she whispered, feeling the darkness form a cloak around them, not just hiding them from anyone passing along the street, but enfolding them into an intimate cocoon of darkness.

"Yeah. That's so," he teased, lowering his head, but he didn't kiss her. Not yet. Again, she felt the evidence of his arousal. It was almost instantaneous, which gave her a surge of power, of sexual confidence that she'd never felt before. Never had she had this strong of an impact on a man and it was a heady experience.

"So...are ye gonna drive me home?" she whispered, their lips hovering so close, but not close enough.

"Aye." His warm breath washed over her face, his fingers tightening on her waist. "Eventually."

She smiled, feeling that surge of power intensify. "Whot's holding ye back?" They were no longer talking about him driving her back to the castle. Her question was all about the here and now.

The challenge worked. He lowered his mouth to hers and...explosion was too mild a term for her reaction. Even knowing how incendiary his kiss could be, she still wasn't prepared for her reaction.

Swiftly, she lifted up onto her toes, deepening the kiss, the connection. She felt her breasts brush against his chest and heard a sound. That might have come from her, or it could have been from Callum. She didn't know, nor did she care. Her only thought was that she needed to be closer. Closer to this man and closer to whatever promise this kiss portended.

Her hands moved, sliding over tense muscles, her fingertips exploring as her mind whirled. Her mouth opened and her tongue mated with his. They knew what to do now. She understood where this kiss was heading even if her mind wasn't functioning with enough...any...clarity at the moment. Instinctively, she raised her arms, her fingers finding the warm, bare skin along his neck, seeking out that warmth and absorbing it into the tips of her fingers. The heat, bubbled inside of her, pooling in that secret spot low in her belly, throbbing with anticipation.

The knocking on the garage door alerted them to someone else's presence.

They drew apart, breathing heavily as they stared into each other's eyes for a long moment. She felt Callum's fingers tighten on her back, almost as if he wanted to ignore the interruption. As if he were contemplating carrying her out of the garage and into his bedroom. Or even better, lifting her onto the hood of the sedan behind her.

Both options appealed to her. A bedroom would allow more time to explore and more comfort during that exploration. But the hood of his car was right here! It was ready for them and they wouldn't need to go anywhere. It was deliciously possible and close!

"Fiona!" the voice called again, coming from a different angle. The voice was familiar for some reason, but her mind couldn't process the voice or the familiarity. Not yet. Not with his hands smoothing against her back in that sensuous way.

"Your father," Callum growled.

That jerked her back to the present. Reality wasn't as nice, but she pulled away, straightening her clothing. Startled by that realization, she looked up at Callum in the dim light coming in through the small window. "Were you...?"

"Fiona! Are you here?" her father yelled yet again.

She pressed her lips together, not bothering to finish the question. Because of course he had. His sneaky hands had slipped under her blue sweater. She remembered the heat of his touch and her body melted, her eyes moving back to his open shirt.

At her look, he began to button the shirt and Fiona found herself glaring at those fingers that were slowly veiling his tanned chest from view.

He chuckled softly and her eyes lifted. "Later," he promised.

Fiona's cheeks heated and she turned away, embarrassed to have been so brazen. "Right," she sighed, patting her hair to ensure that it was still modestly pulled back. There were a few strands that had escaped, but she didn't have a mirror to see what she looked like.

"Ye look bonny, Fi."

She turned, glancing at him over her shoulder. He must have read the worry in her eyes because he shook his head. "Nay, ye dinna look as if some obnoxious man nearly made love to you against the side of a car."

Her mouth fell open and she glanced back at the car. But she wasn't shocked at the idea of having sex out here. She was wondering about the mechanics of having sex against the side of a car versus on the hood. Both ideas were...tempting! Too tempting.

Turning away from the images of the car and Callum doing naughty things to her against the car, she forced her feet to move forward. She stepped through the doorway to find her father peering through cupped hands in the windows.

"Father? Wha' are ye doing?"

Abruptly, Duncan pulled away, dropping his hands to his sides and trying to act like he hadn't just been acting like a peeping tom.

"Fiona!" her father gasped, for once looking flustered. But he rallied quickly, his normal "performance mode" kicking in as soon as Callum stepped out of the garage behind her. "I was looking for you!" His brogue was completely hidden now.

Her head tilted. "Why? Ye've never concerned yerself with me comings and goings afore."

Again, he looked startled at her push back. "You're my daughter!" he replied, his British accent deepening. "I am always concerned about you, dear."

Last night at the pub, her father had been completely Scottish and the accent was heavily in play. But now, in front of Callum who everyone assumed hailed from the United States, the man's accent as a very upper-class British. Because Americans admired anyone with a British accent? Fiona suspected that her father was trying to impress Callum, which made her stomach tighten with dread. Callum was to be her father's next victim! He wasn't staying around because she wouldn't give him more money. Well, not anymore. Duncan must have seen Callum at the pub last night and asked about him.

Callum was well dressed in obviously expensive clothing, so it would make sense that he appeared to be an excellent candidate for Duncan's next scam. But Fiona couldn't let her father do that! Not to Callum. Yes, Callum was smart and savvy. He was obviously a wealthy businessman. But her father knew the tricks, knew how to twist his comments and ply his charm so that even his worst enemy would think that they were best friends!

"Ye've never been concerned about me afore, Father." She crossed her arms over her stomach and glared at him.

"Of course I'm concerned with ye, lass." The fact that his brogue came out right then revealed Fiona had startled him. He pulled himself together, snapping his expensive, most likely hand-tailored jacket together in a quick jerk of indignation. "I'm always concerned with you." And the brogue vanished again. "Isn't that the whole reason why I go to London? To help you ferret out excellent business deals?" He smiled over her shoulder, obviously trying to charm Callum. "My daughter and I are business partners, you see. I find good deals in which she can invest our money."

"We're not..." she stopped when she felt Callum's hand on her back. "I'm fine, Father. Thank you for your concern." She changed her statement at his touch, remembering that they couldn't afford to alienate him. Not yet. They had a plan. She needed to pull back on her cold treatment of the man. For now.

"I'm going to drive Fiona home now," Callum told the older man. "If there's nothing else?"

Duncan blinked, his gaze moving from Fiona to Callum, then back again. "No." he replied, a slow, mercenary smile forming on his blandly handsome features. "Nothing else. You two go. Have fun." He chuckled, shaking his head as he walked back up the path towards the road. "But not too much fun, mind ye!" he called back over his shoulder, as he hurried off down the street.

They both waited, watching, until her father rounded the corner and vanished behind the craggy rocks and tall grass. When he was out of sight, she sighed and looked up at Callum.

"He's put you on his radar."

Callum nodded, still watching the direction in which the older man had disappeared. "I agree." He looked down at her. "I'll be on my guard."

She sighed, relieved that he'd grasped her father's mercenary intentions as well. "Good. Now I really need te get back. Ah have a meeting in a few minutes." She patted her denim clad thighs. "Would ye mind driving me back? I can walk if ye're busy."

"Not a chance," he growled, then put his hand on the small of her back, guiding her into the garage once more. "I don't trust yer father te not try te murder ye again."

He'd just pulled open the door to the passenger side of his sleek, black sedan and she looked up at him. "Who said anything about murder?"

His lips twisted into a grimace. "I think yer father cut the brake lines on yer car. When I looked at the lines, there were slices, not normal wear and tear. Driving over a rock or debris didn't damage the brake line. Someone cut them."

Startled, she gripped the door. "Nay!"

"Aye."

She couldn't believe that. Not because she didn't believe him about the cut lines versus the torn lines, but because she simply couldn't believe that someone would try to kill her. "Nay!"

He reached out, his hand cupping her neck. "Believe it, Fi," he told her firmly. "The brake lines were cut and it was recent. There's no corrosion along the edges. That's why I asked who had access yer car. Because someone cut the lines, probably hoping tha' ye would be traveling through the other side o' the village, the side where the road is steep and the cliffs along the street's tight corners are covered in rocks."

"Nay!" she hissed again. "Ah canna believe that!"

"Ah dinna ken anything fer sure. But tha's why I want te have a different mechanic look at yer car. I'm sure that yer mechanic is good, but I want a forensic person te take a look and see if there's some evidence left over from whoever cut the lines." He stared at her for a long moment before he continued. "Will ye trust me?"

She thought about it for a long moment, then nodded. "Aye."

She slipped into the sedan then, her knees trembling too much to continue holding her upright. The soft leather of his car's passenger seat was a welcome relief.

Grinding his teeth, he shifted so that the old, stone fence hid him more thoroughly, tracking the black sedan's movements with binoculars. Why the hell had Fiona broken her usual routine and driven this way? The roads on this side of the village weren't nearly as steep! The damn woman had messed with his plans. If she'd followed her normal routine, then she'd be at the bottom of a rocky ravine right now. And because those cliffs were so steep, the crash, as well as her body, wouldn't have been discovered for a long time! Everyone in the village would have just assumed that she'd gone on a trip.

Of course, he would have mentioned that Fiona had "planned" a trip to some place outside of the village to anyone who would listen, just to ensure that no one went looking for her. And dammit, that bastard had been under the car so he must know that the brake lines had been cut with a knife. If Fiona had just followed her normal routine and gone into the village like a good girl, the crash would have hidden the cleanly severed brake lines. That's only if someone had thought about investigating a car crash along these narrow, winding roads.

Dammit, his "perfect plans" were turning out to be not so perfect! But he needed to get her out of the way so he could properly search the castle!

Leaning back slightly, he lowered the binoculars and contemplated his next move. This wasn't the end, he told himself with renewed optimism. Just another setback. Obviously, he needed to plan more carefully, take into account every possibility so his next plan would be successful. There were other ways to get rid of the woman who stood in the way of his freedom! He was creative and determined! So what if his first two attempts had failed? He was nothing if not single-minded.

Chapter 4

"Fiona!"

Swallowing a groan, Fiona turned and plastered on a polite smile. "Good morning, Bernard. How are ye doing on this fine mornin?" she asked, gripping the grocery basket with both hands in front of her like a shield. She'd learned the hard way that Bernard was a hugger. And a creepy one at that! His hugs weren't the polite, friendly kind. Nope, the guy lingered and let his hands wander. He pressed his groin against her stomach and...ick. He was just gross.

Looking into his watery, blue eyes, she saw surprise lurking there. What an odd reaction. Granted, it was later in the week than she normally shopped. She'd come to the grocery store today instead of her normal shopping day specifically to avoid him and his creepy hugs.

Sure enough, Bernard leaned forward, reaching for a hug, but Fiona shifted the grocery basket between them and extended her hand instead. Bernard blinked at the obstacle, then looked up at her as if she'd just insulted him somehow. But he took her hand in his and she managed not to shudder at the man's sweaty grasp.

Fiona pulled her hand quickly away, fighting back the urge to wipe it on her jeans. "Good te see ye, Bernard," she said and started to move away.

Bernard seemed to inhale, then he shifted his roundish body so that he was still blocking her path. "I heard that you were in an accident yesterday. I wanted to make sure that you were okay." Again, he started to lean forward, determined to hug her.

But Fiona was done with the subtle hints. This time, she stepped back, raising the grocery basket higher and putting a hand up to ward him off. "Bernard, I dinna like being hugged."

The hurt in his eyes made her feel a touch guilty, but she straightened her shoulders against the feeling and stared right back at the man. He was *trying* to make her feel guilty, the jerk!

That became even more evident when his "sad" expression cleared and he shuffled his heavy, cowboy boot covered feet. Why cowboy boots? This was Scotland! Not the American west! He'd paired the cowboy boots with dress slacks and, in Fiona's opinion, that look only worked when a man was tall, muscular, and confident. Bernard wasn't any of those things. He was maybe an inch taller than her, carried an extra fifty pounds, most of which was centered around his waist, and the only time he was confident was when he was trying to weasel his way into her life.

"Well, it's actually perfect timing, running into you like this. I was hoping that maybe we could get that cup of coffee we've talked about or, even better, you could join me for dinner some night! We've been trying for months now, ever since I moved into the village. Our schedules," he sighed, shaking his head as if they were both so busy, "well, we just have so many obligations."

What obligations? According to the village gossip, the man had inherited a vast amount of money from his family and didn't work. He didn't volunteer his time or expertise, not that he had any expertise, since he'd never worked a day in his life. And he didn't have any hobbies that anyone knew about. His yard was a wasteland of weeds so he didn't garden and his house...it was small but tidy. Not large enough to take up most of his spare hours. So, what did the man actually do all day, besides try to corner her at the shop?

She didn't know, nor did she care to find out.

"Ah'm sorry, Bernard, but I dinna have time today. Ah'm meeting some friends at the pub tonight te play poker."

"Oh, I'd love to come!" he replied, brightening and clapping his hands. "Thank you for mentioning it. It just so happens I have an opening in my schedule!"

Fiona opened her mouth to tell him that he wasn't invited, but stopped herself. If Bernard wanted to play poker with her and Callum, then she didn't mind winning some of his lauded inheritance. The man was an annoying gnat who couldn't take a hint, and apparently, he couldn't comprehend an explicit "no" either.

"A small group o' us are playing poker over at Aurthur's pub. If ye'd like te join, we're meeting up at seven o'clock. Bring cash."

"Oh, this is...uh, *real* poker?" he asked, hesitating for a moment.

"Aye. The people coming tonight play fer keeps." She softened her tone. "Unless ye don't ken how to play poker? I'd understand if this isna ye're cup o' tea, Bernard."

He looked flustered for a moment, his ruddy cheeks highlighting the blush. "Oh, no! I know how to play poker, my dear. Absolutely! I'm very good at poker!" He chuckled slightly, still rubbing his fleshy hands together.

Fiona felt Callum's presence before he came around the corner, his grocery cart filled with various appetizers. He'd selected some gourmet cheese and crusty bread, as well as several varieties of crackers. He'd also included pre-baked cakes and brownies, some chips and dips. The man might have gone a bit overboard, but she forgave him when he slipped his arm around her waist. The silent message was for Bernard, a territorial warning from one male to another. It was a typical male gesture that would have irritated Fiona, if Bernard's eyes hadn't bugged out with abrupt understanding. A claim had been made and Bernard was out in the cold.

"Oh, I say..." he paused, his lips pressing together. "Fiona, why don't ye introduce me te your...brother? For some reason, I assumed that you were the only child of Duncan's. But apparently...."

"This isna me brother," she replied. "Yer assumption was correct. Ah'm an only child." She leaned into Callum and he tightened his grip around her. He even pressed a kiss to the top of her head, just in case Bernard didn't grasp the full meaning of Callum's arm around her waist.

Bernard's eyes narrowed and, for the first time, Fiona felt a twinge of worry. Bernard was normally annoying, no matter how firmly she rejected his advances. But now, she couldn't miss the fury in those beady eyes. She actually moved closer to Callum and, in that second, Bernard's eyes cleared and he reverted back to the kind, older gentleman that seemed clueless but not dangerous.

"Well! I say, a good game of poker sounds like just the thing to break up the monotony of one's life, eh?"

Just as had happened yesterday with her father, the Scottish brogue dissipated, to be replaced by a British accent. While her father's British accent was an affectation, Fiona suddenly suspected that Bernard's was genuine and his brogue was faked.

How odd! But then, he'd been an odd duck since moving into the village several months earlier.

"Well, I'll be on my way then!" he called out, the brogue firmly back in place. "Until tonight, my dear!"

He bustled off down the aisle. He turned and glanced back at them, but when he realized they were still watching him, he hurried out of the store, setting his wire basket down just outside the door, completely unaware of Megan, the cashier, who glared at the man's retreating back, then down at the groceries that she'd have to return to the shelves.

"That was odd," Fiona commented. "Did ye notice...?"

"His changing accent?" Callum filled in when she trailed off. "Aye. I got that."

She looked up at him, noticed that his eyes were narrowed as he continued to watch the man. "Oh, dinna worry about Bernard. He's nice enough, bu' completely clueless."

"An' ye invited him te play poker tenight wi' us?"

She cringed, then her smile turned evil. "No' exactly. I mentioned the poker game tonight and Bernard invited himself. He's been asking me oot er' since he moved te the village. He refuses to believe I'm no' interested."

Callum looked down at her, his dark eyes narrowing dangerously. "He's asked ye oot?"

"Aye. Coffee, tea, dinner, brunch." She shrugged. "The man is persistent, I'll gi' him tha'."

Callum watched Bernard turn the corner and vanish from view in disgust. "The man is more than fifty years old!" he growled, taking the basket from her and putting it in his grocery cart.

"It isna the age difference tha' bothers me so much," she explained as they walked together towards the cashier. "It's his attitude. He acts as if Ah owe him a date." She glanced out the store windows. "And more. Sometimes, I feel as if he expects...well, let's just say that he parades his inheritance around the village like he is entitled te more than wha' the villagers are willing to give."

"He doesna work?"

She shrugged, taking items from the cart and placing them on the conveyor belt for Megan. "Not tha' any o' us know about. He's just...a trust fund, frat boy tha' ne'er actually grew up."

Callum snorted, and helped Fiona load up the groceries. Fiona tried to pay, but Callum simply walked behind her, wrapped his arms "lovingly" around her waist and slid his own credit card into the slot instead.

"I was going to-"

"I know," he replied, then kissed the nape of her neck. When Fiona looked up, the cashier was blushing as she smiled shyly at them, handing over the paper bags filled with their groceries.

"Let's head o'er te the pub te set up the back room," he suggested.

Fiona walked beside him, wondering what Callum's ultimate goal was. He'd driven her home yesterday morning, then left her at the door with a sweet, gentle kiss that had curled her toes. Then today, he'd arrived at the castle early, explaining that his friends had agreed to help with the poker games and that they needed to start the poker games with the villagers in order to bait the hook, as he'd so eloquently explained. That was why they'd made a trip to the grocery store to stock up on appetizers.

"Why did we need fruit, cheese, crackers, and chips fer tonight? Arthur would have provided anything we need."

"Arthur will provide the alcohol. But no way am I trusting him wi' the food," he replied with a grim set to his jawline.

She smiled, leaning her head against his shoulder in support. "I'm so sorry tha' ye grew up hating stew. Because Arthur's really is quite delicious."

He grunted, heading in the direction of the pub. "I know a woman who was required to always eat her vegetables as a kid." He turned a corner and accelerated. "If she didna eat her vegetables fer dinner, her father would put them into the fridge and serve them te her fer breakfast. She wasna allowed to get up from the table until she'd eaten them."

"Is this actually ye?"

He glanced at her, his gaze clear he wasn't lying.

"Sorry," she replied, trying to smother a smile. "Please," she said, waving her hand in the air. "Continue."

"The girl had a sister in the same situation. One night, they were served lima beans for dinner. Neither o' them wanted te eat their lima beans."

Fiona shuddered in horror. "I dinna blame them. Lima beans are disgusting."

"The father put the lima beans inte the fridge. They were brought oot again the following morning for breakfast. The older sister tried to stuff the lima beans into her mouth so she could just get it o'er with."

"Is this a current friend o' yers?"

"Dinna interrupt." He turned right and parked in the pub's small parking lot. Shutting off the engine, he turned and looked at her. "The older sister gagged on the lima beans. She threw up all o'er her plate and the father let her give up on eating the rest o' her lima beans. But the younger sister had te remain at the table and finish all of her own lima beans."

Fiona shuddered. "That sounds horrible!"

"Te this day, the younger girl gags whenever she tries to eat vegetables. She associates lima beans and a whole host of o'er vegetables wi' throwing up."

Fiona nodded, lifting her hand to run a finger along his jaw. "Tha's the same reaction ye have to stew, right?"

"Aye."

For a long moment, she gazed up at him, awed. He'd overcome so many obstacles to become who he is now. He was a strong, vital, powerful man who had conquered his industry. He was a leader in the property development world and people in so many other industries respected him. No one messed with Callum MacGreggor.

And yet, here he was, setting up a poker game in a small village in Scotland. What was it about Callum that...spoke to her? No, that wasn't quite the right question. What was it about him that called to her? He was strong and powerful, but many men were. She'd met many men during her years at university and in her business interactions over the years. None of them were as compelling, as magnetically appealing, as Callum.

"I want ye," she blurted out. Then pulled back, shocked that she'd admitted it out loud.

Callum's gaze heated up. "I want ye too," he replied, reaching up and holding her hand against his jaw when she would have pulled away. "I dinna think that I can wait until this business with your father is o'er, Fi," he warned. "I couldna sleep last night, thinking aboot kissing ye. Making love to ye."

She held her breath, shocked that he would be so blatant about his desires. She'd grown up learning to hide her hopes and dreams, her fantasies. But Callum's ability to simply state what he wanted helped her to be just as open.

She swallowed, her fingers sliding over his skin. "I dinna think ah want te wait that long either." She leaned forward, unconcerned about being seen. "I feel as if I've been asleep fer so long, and then ye come into my life an' woke me up." She kissed him again. "Tha's no' fair. Because ye're gonna leave an' I'll be stuck here."

He opened his mouth to argue, but she didn't want to hear false promises. She didn't need that from him. She needed honesty and sex. A lot of sex! Tonight, she vowed she was going to discover what sex was like with Callum.

"How long do ye think the poker game will last tonight?" he growled, his hands tightening on her waist.

She laughed softly, her eyes sparkling with humor. "The villagers here dinna generally stay up much later than nine o'clock. I would expect most o' them would be ready te head oot around eight."

"Excellent," he whispered into her ear. "Then we'll pick this up again a' eight."

It wasn't a question. It was a statement. A command. His tone had anticipation shooting through her body and she shivered, nodding her agreement. "Eight o'clock," she replied.

"Let's unload the groceries an' get e'erything set up. Then we'll play a few hands o' poker, just the two o' us, just fer fun."

She climbed out of the car but paused, looking at him over the top of the sedan. "We're still going te let the other villagers win tonight, aye?"

"All o' them will come away wi' more money than they started, with the exception o' yer old friend, Mr. Bernard." He slammed the driver's door closed. "That man's gonna lose e'ery dime he started wi'."

She laughed, meeting him at the back of his sedan. "Ah like the way ye think!"

They pulled the grocery bags from the trunk and walked into the pub. Arthur greeted them heartily, waving them towards the back room where he held private parties. There wasn't much need for a private party room in the village. Those kinds of rooms were reserved for weddings or funerals, or other significant life events. When those happened, most of the time, the whole village was invited. But the room harkened back to the time period when ladies who dared to travel outside of their own sphere, were given private rooms, away from the riff raff of society. Most of the time, the room was used for storage. But it was perfect for their purposes.

Over the next few hours, she and Callum, along with Arthur and Sorcha, worked to clean out the room and set up several round tables with six chairs surrounding each. They also put out a long, rectangular table for the snacks and Sorcha insisted it needed a tablecloth.

The whole atmosphere was one of anticipation, the four of them laughing and...well, three of them laughing. Callum smiled occasionally. But he generally kept well away from the others. Fiona didn't understand, but respected his need to observe more than participate.

The bastards thought they could hide from him? No, not hide. They thought they could invite everyone but him to their party! Well, he'd show them! He'd show up and they'd have to let him participate in whatever they were planning! He knotted his tie and buttoned his vest. He'd paid a pretty penny for this outfit. But he needed to impress. The people around here were stupid! They loved the finery and baubles that came with wealth. So he'd give them the show they were expecting.

What they didn't know was that he had bigger, better plans than to hang out in this damn village for the rest of his life! No way! He had big plans! Better plans!

And it all started with getting rid of that bitch. As soon as Fiona Reid was out of the picture, he'd have complete freedom. His future would be secure!

He chuckled, smoothing a hand over the fine wool of his jacket. Fiona looked down on him. Little did she know that he would be looking down on her. In a most literal sense! Very soon! He had a new plan. Cutting the brake lines had been too easy. There had been too many ways in which he could have been caught.

No, his next plan would be better. Safer and more effective.

Chapter 5

The evening was a resounding success! There hadn't been just one table of poker players. As soon as the other villagers wandered into the pub, several more wanted to play as well. Even Father Finn had joined in, laughing whether he won or lost.

Because so many of the villagers wanted to join in, they'd expanded to five tables, six players each. It also helped that Fiona had told Arthur to charge all of the ale and beers to her, allowing the alcohol to flow more easily.

They'd moved out of the private room that they'd initially set up because there just wasn't enough room for all of the players, as well as the villagers who wanted to watch, so they kept the food and snacks there, allowing everyone to wander in and out at will.

Bernard nearly shoved one of the older residents out of the way in order to sit at what he called "the high table". Neither Callum nor Fiona argued with him. Father Finn even participated, abandoning his priestly garb and wearing a fine, wool jacket. "Better to not sully the vestments with gambling," he told the group with a chuckle.

Although her father didn't deign to participate, Duncan showed up in a plaid kilt with matching wool jacket, acting as if he were laird of the manor. Fiona wondered how much that suit had cost her. She knew that her father didn't actually work, so everything he wore, everything he ate and drank, would be charged to her account. She just hoped that he didn't get drunk tonight. With a pint of ale in his hands at all times, Duncan sat on a bar stool, commenting on the strategy of the players. He was annoying, but Fiona and Callum knew that he was doing exactly what they needed him to do; observing and acting superior.

Fiona and Callum sat with Bernard and three others from the village. Initially, Bernard shuffled the cards like a pro and Fiona worried that he might actually know how to play poker well enough to challenge them. That would be bad, since their strategy was to rid the man of every dime he'd brought to the table.

But it turned out that the man was all flair and no substance. Fiona ensured that the others at the table occasionally won a few hands, lost a few, but came out relatively even by the end of the night. But whenever Bernard started tossing money around, he was so easy to read. She knew exactly when he was bluffing and when he actually had a good hand. Towards the end of the evening, he was flushed, sweaty, and huffing like he was struggling to breathe.

"Are ye okay, Bernard?" she asked solicitously, noticing that they were the last table still playing. As predicted, it was eight thirty and most of the others had departed for their beds. It was just her, Bernard, and Callum with her father and two of the older ladies. Father Finn slipped in and out from the tables, helping Arthur clean up and keeping up a light conversation.

"I'm fine!" Bernard snapped, blotting his forehead with his sleeve. It came away with a sweat mark, not that Bernard bothered to notice. The wool jacket had long been abandoned, but that wasn't unusual since everyone's wool jackets and vests had been removed. The pub really was quite stuffy tonight.

"Are ye sure ye want te play another hand?" Fiona asked, trying to keep her tone sweet and innocent.

Bernard looked at Fiona, then at Callum, then at the stacks of chips in front of each of them, and then at the three chips left before him. With a growl, he grabbed his remaining chips and stormed out of the pub.

There was a moment of surprised silence after his departure. Finally, Father Finn broke in with "Well, that was abrupt!"

"Goodness, Ah've ne'er seen Bernard so huffy!" Sorcha huffed.

The door to the pub opened again and the man in question stood there, almost trembling with rage.

He bowed slightly, his eyes looking beady in his swollen features. "Fiona, could I have a private word with you?"

Silence greeted his request. Fiona felt everyone's eyes on her, waiting for her reaction. Slowly, she took in a deep breath, then nodded a jerky agreement.

"Nay."

Callum stepped in front of her, guarding her from Bernard's anger.

Fiona's heart soared with...gratitude? Someone was standing up...for her? Someone was looking out for her? She couldn't remember that happening...ever!

She moved closer to him, placing a hand on his arm and he instantly jerked his gaze down to her. "It's okay."

"Nay. He's angry aboot something and we dinna know wha' he'll do."

She smiled softly up at him. "It's better te know wha's on his mind, isna it? Better to be aware than guessing."

Callum stared down at Fiona, her pale skin almost glowing in the dim light of the pub. He didn't understand how that could happen. Her skin should look darker, less alive and beautiful. But it seemed that everything about Fiona had a happy glow right now. And that happiness soothed the beast inside of him. That beast had been clawing at his gut for years, needing retribution for the grievances of his past. So how could a simple touch calm that beast and ease the gnawing ache inside of him?

"Ah'll be right back," she whispered.

Callum watched her move towards Bernard, who was obviously clearly upset about losing in such a public forum. Bernard liked to pretend that he was smarter and more savvy than the other villagers. Everyone in the village would be gossiping about his losses by tomorrow, and he knew it.

Fiona nodded to Bernard, who still stood in the doorway, waiting for her. There was something off about him. Callum made a mental note to ask Dash to look into him. It was time to do a bit more digging into the residents. There were just too many inconsistencies. He hesitated to call them lies. But the facts and actions of a few of the residents didn't add up.

He watched Fiona step through the door with the man that seemed to irritate everyone. Callum silently debated staying inside, allowing the two a private word. But every protective instinct inside of him screamed to follow, to ensure that Fiona was safe.

So instead of holding back, he strode out through the heavy door of the pub and looked around, spotting Bernard and Fiona off to the side. Both of them glanced in his direction, but only Fiona smiled at him. Bernard glared, silently demanding that Callum go back inside.

He ignored the short faker.

"Faker"? Now why did that term spring to mind when he thought of Bernard?

Fiona turned slightly, facing Bernard. She wanted to hear what he had to say and get back inside. No, that wasn't completely accurate. She wanted to slide into Callum's arms and hug him tightly. She wanted to feel the heat of his body against hers. She wanted to...make love with him. Tonight! It was late and the night was deeply dark. So, why wasn't she in a rush to get back to the castle? Why wasn't she thinking about work? She had company reports to read through and decisions to make. She needed to check the U.S. stock market, which would be closing soon, and perhaps shift some of her investments. Maybe buy stock in that company she'd heard such great things about.

She had a list of issues to deal with in her office in the left wing of the castle. So, why was her body coming alive simply because a tall, handsome man stepped into the darkness to watch out for her? She could take care of herself. She wasn't defenseless.

But goodness it felt wonderful to not *have* to do everything on her own! It felt amazing to know that someone had her back.

Callum stood off to the side, his big, muscular arms crossed over his chest. He didn't come any closer, but his presence obviously irritated Bernard. Good! The guy was weird and didn't respect personal boundaries.

"What did you need to tell me, Bernard?" she prompted, pulling the man's beady-eyed glare back to her.

The man sighed, shifted on his feet once again, then started speaking. "I understand that you have..." he stopped, pressing his lips thoughtfully together for a moment. Then he continued. "I know that you are young and have needs, Fiona. Physical needs. And although I would prefer that you come to me for those needs," he shot a fulminating glare at Callum and sighed, "there is also the appeal of a more...basic man. You are young and have more...physical...needs that need to be fulfilled." He wrinkled his nose in obvious distaste. "Therefore, I will allow you to spend some time with that...Neanderthal." He lifted his gaze to meet hers, not registering the shock and revulsion in her face now. "However, I also know that you crave a more intellectual connection for your life partner. So, go ahead. Have your affair. When you have worked him out of your system, then I will be waiting and we can negotiate our new life together."

With that, Bernard turned on his heel and strode off down the street. Before he left the circle of light cast by the pub's parking lot lights, she saw him tug at his wool jacket in a haughty, put-upon manner.

Fiona stood there, stunned. She wasn't sure if she should laugh, or become furiously, righteously outraged.

She turned to find Callum standing close by. "Did you hear that?"

"Not all of it," he replied, wrapping his arm around her shoulders to guide her back inside. "What did he say?"

She huffed a bit, walking beside him. "He said that he understood that I was young and..." she huffed a bit. "Well, he basically told me to have sex with ye an' get ye oot o' my system so that I can return te him and spend the rest o' my life with his creepy self."

Callum stopped, gaping down at her. "Are ye serious?"

"Yep!" she confirmed, adding a nod, then turning to glare into the darkness that had absorbed the creep. "What nerve! He said that I need an intellectual connection and that when I'm done wi' you, then he and I can 'negotiate' our future together." She shuddered. "Not in this, or *any*, lifetime!"

Fiona jerked the door open and stepped back into the warmth of the pub. She stomped around, collecting bits and pieces, trying to help Arthur and Sorcha clean up. Her father was still sitting off to the side, scrolling through something on his phone. He would never deign to clean up after a party. That would be beneath him. But Father Finn was still here and he did help. Father Finn was the only other person who noticed her anger and came closer.

"Would ye like me to speak to the mon, lass?" he offered. "He's a bit thick in the head, but I can probably get through te him."

Fiona smiled gratefully, but shook her head. "Thank ye, Father Finn. But that's a conversation that ah am going to relish having a' some point."

She grabbed the last few glasses and brought them to the bar where Arthur would wash them up. Overall, the night had been a success. She estimated that she'd won about two thousand pounds away from Bernard, while adding two or three hundred pounds to the piles of their other players. Sorcha had collected all of the initial cash, converting each player's cash to poker chips, then converting them back into cash at the end of the evening. Arthur tallied up the total for the drinks and Fiona paid for everything with her winnings, soothing her temper with the realization that Bernard had paid for the villagers' drinks that night.

"Well, I guess that's it then!" her father announced, standing up and grabbing his jacket. He didn't bother to put it on. Instead, he draped it over his arm and grabbed his hat. He didn't look around to wait for her. He simply walked out into the night.

Father Finn followed, leaving Fiona and Callum alone among the tables.

She stared up at him, her heart hammering against her ribs. "Well, should we...?"

"Head back to my place," he finished for her, moving closer and taking her hands in his. "Will ye come with me?"

Fiona didn't need to think about it. She'd been thinking about little else all day. "Yes," she replied, stepping closer and tilting her head back. "I'd like that very much."

He shifted so that his big body shielded her from the bar area, not that

Arthur and Sorcha were around. They'd disappeared, providing a bit of privacy. "Let's go," he growled.

He turned, still holding her hand and collected their jackets. "Thank you, Arthur and Sorcha! Tonight was wonderful!" Fiona called out a moment before Callum practically dragged her out into the night.

His car was the only one still parked in the lot. He courteously opened the passenger seat door for her. He paused, looking like he was going to kiss her. But he shook his head. "No, if I kiss you here, we'll ne'er reach a bed."

Fiona felt like laughing as she ducked into the passenger seat and pulled the door closed, watching with hungry eyes as he walked around the front of the car to the driver's side.

He glared at the taillights as they slowly faded into the distance. With an angry jerk, he snapped the top back onto the syringe.

"Another night," he vowed, slipping the GHB filled syringe back into his pocket. He'd tried several times to dump the stuff into Fiona during the night. It would have been better if the other villagers had seen her and thought she'd gotten drunk. No one would have questioned him if he'd led her out of the pub and walked her home.

Well, the big guy might have. He hadn't realized that MacGreggor was going to be a major part of the evening. So, perhaps it was better that he hadn't injected Fiona tonight. MacGreggor would have tried to take care of her and...well, that wasn't part of his plan.

Nor was Fiona driving away. She was supposed to walk back up to the castle, damn it! She was supposed to be alone on a dark, lonely road!

Grinding his teeth, he walked back to his place, scrabbling for a new plan. He could still use the GHB, but he'd have to be subtler. Obviously, Fiona's regular daily patterns were all shot to hell now that MacGreggor was in town. It wouldn't be a problem, though. He was smart and flexible. He'd survived this long by staying on his toes. He just needed that woman out of the way! Then he could get what he needed and his life would be so much better.

He muttered several choice expletives as he stepped out of his hiding place. But moments later, he dove back behind the stone fence as headlights rounded the corner. He hadn't expected anyone to be out this late.

Heart pounding, he waited several long minutes, after the sound of the car's engine faded away.

Had he been seen? Surely not. If they'd seen him dive behind the wall, they would have stopped. Because of the way he dove, it probably looked like he'd fallen. So, if someone had seen him, they would have assumed that he'd fallen and would have stopped to check on him. That was the neighborly thing to do. It wasn't like he was a stranger to these parts. Everyone in the village knew him. They would have stopped, offered help.

So no, he was safe. No one saw him hiding and no one witnessed his dive back to his hiding place.

Dusting off his slacks, he moved back down to the sidewalk. Whistling, trying to appear casual just in case someone else drove by, he slid his hands into his pockets, his fingers fiddling with the syringe as he came up with a new plan. She was surprisingly difficult to get rid of!

Chapter 6

It took Callum less than five minutes to reach his rented cottage. As soon as he pulled into the garage, silence descended around them. They both climbed out of the vehicle, the overhead light still on. In a blink, Callum was around to Fiona's side of the car, leading her into the house. He'd left several lights on inside, so they weren't in complete darkness.

"What do I do?" she whispered, unwilling to break the spell of the night.

"Ye should kiss me," he replied, one arm wrapping around her waist, pulling her against his body.

"I can do that," Fiona replied, her heart pounding against her ribs.

"I know ye can," he agreed and lowered his head to initiate the kiss. The caress started off slow and gentle, but quickly escalated as their combined passion ignited. The kiss turned into something more, something powerful. She whimpered when he lifted his mouth, but Fiona discovered that the cessation was merely so that he could lift her into his arms. She wrapped her arms around his neck as he carried her up the stairs, into his bedroom. He kicked the door closed behind them, but didn't halt until they were right next to the bed. Only then did he release her, barely allowing her feet to touch the floor as he started kissing her again.

Her hands moved over his shoulders, his arms, and then back up, touching the soft hair at the nape of his neck. "Can I...take yer shirt off?" she asked as she fumbled with the buttons on his dress shirt.

In response, he stepped back, unbuttoning the first few buttons, then simply pulled the shirt over his head, dumping it on the floor. "Touch me, Fi," he urged, pressing her to his bare chest. Almost overwhelmed, Callum closed his eyes, allowing the intense pleasure to wash over him. Her fingers moved, sliding over his skin, exploring and tempting, taunting him, driving him wild.

"Ye're so amazing," she whispered.

His hands clenched at her waist, trying to slow down so that he could focus on enjoying the rush of sensations. But it was difficult. Fiona's fingers were light and delicate, teasing his skin, making his mind race to the moment when he could finally...!

"I need ye naked," he warned as he pulled her sweater up and over her head, dumping it on top of his dress shirt. He heard her gasp, but he didn't slow down. He had to see her, had to feel all of that pale, delicate skin that had been taunting him for days.

He heard her gasp when his hands slid over that skin, which was softer than he'd anticipated. So incredibly soft and pale and perfect!

His hands skimmed across her skin, testing, tempting, as Fiona gasped and shivered in response. His hands were hot, heating up her skin like nothing she'd ever experienced before. "This is–"

"Too much," he finished for her as her own fingers left a trail of fire down over his chest. She didn't stop until her fingers found his belt. With a groan, he whipped the belt away, then tugged off his slacks and boxers, leaving him completely naked before her.

"Ye're..." she stopped, stunned when he dropped to his knees in front of her. She watched breathlessly as he reached up, his fingers deftly releasing the snap on her jeans, then slowly, tauntingly, pulling the zipper down.

She held her breath, entirely focused on his long fingers, staring into his dark eyes as he tugged her jeans down her legs. He paused to admire the picture she made in white, satin panties. Fiona heard a slight growl, but her mind couldn't register the sound, couldn't make sense of it, because his mouth was there, at the apex of her thighs. His tongue darted out, but the satin stopped any direct contact.

Fiona whimpered, needing everything gone, every obstacle out of the way. She'd never felt this...crazed. She wanted to pull back because his touches were too much, overwhelmingly intense. And yet, she also wanted to scream and rip the material out of the way so that his mouth was against her body!

"This has to go," he grumbled, his fingers looping around the waistband of her panties. A moment later, they were gone and Callum tossed them out of the way. In the back of her mind, Fiona reminded herself to look at where they fell because she'd need those panties later. But before she could finish that thought, his mouth was back, but this time, his lips were directly against her skin.

When his tongue darted out, she whimpered again, her knees quivering as the intensity of that touch, that intimacy struck her. She wanted to spread her legs, but she couldn't.

Somehow, Callum must have realized what was going through her mind because he nudged her backwards on to the bed. Callum's hands moved to her knees, spreading her legs wide. For a long moment, he just stared at her glistening, pink folds, making her body heat up even higher. She was liquid heat in his hands. She was...his head lowered and she held her breath, waiting, her body tightening with anticipation as he kissed the softness of her inner thighs. She spread her legs wider, needing him closer, needing him to kiss her more intimately.

Her fingers dove into his hair, unaware of her fingers directing him, guiding him to that spot that screamed for his touch. When his tongue lapped at her there, she gasped, but her hips rolled, her legs spreading wider to give him better access. He took advantage of her shifting hips, his tongue lapping at that nub while his finger teased the folds, torturing her. It wasn't enough to bring her a climax, but she was so damn close that she wanted to scream!

And then he did it! He sucked on that nub while, at the same time, his finger slid into her heat. Fiona tried desperately to hold back. But the sensations were too much and her body burst into a beautiful, mind-blowing climax that had her back arching, her legs tightening around him as she screamed her pleasure.

She was panting when he stood up and came closer. Fiona watched him and found his impressive shaft was there in front of her. Without thinking, she wrapped her fingers around that shaft, making him to groan. It was such a sexy sound that she did it again, her fingers sliding over his skin, exploring and experimenting.

He growled again, squeezing his eyes closed as he fought to control himself, but Fiona was too fascinated to stop exploring. Her fingers slid against the hardness, her thumb sliding over the top, the tip, just under the ridge. Her other hand moved lower, cupping his softness and learning what that felt like. He was making very odd sounds now, but Fiona ignored them. She'd never particularly cared about male anatomy. Never wondered about a man's parts until she'd met Callum. Now she couldn't seem to get enough of him. She thought she could explore him like this forever, as long as he kept making those sexy sounds.

But too soon, he moved her hands away. He grabbed something out of the bedside drawer and she realized that it was a condom. "Can I?" she asked.

He hesitated, and then nodded sharply. "But hurry, Fi. Ah dinna know how much longer I can last."

Taking the protection in her hands, she eyed it, then looked at his male member, wondering how such a large part of him could fit into such a small piece of latex. She flipped it over, then back again, but her mind simply couldn't figure it out.

In the end, he took the condom back and she watched with fascination as he rolled it down over his shaft. Even then, she wanted to lean forward, to take him into her mouth as he'd done to her. But he pushed her back against the mattress, spreading her legs wider. She wanted this. She wasn't shy any longer. Not with Callum.

"Are ye okay?" he asked. "Tell me te stop."

"Dinna ye dare," she whispered and wrapped her legs around his waist, pulling him in closer.

When Fiona felt that part of him pressing into her, she lifted her hips, needing to feel him. Her breath caught in her throat as he thrust into her, his body filling hers. It felt so tight, so perfect and so...incredibly beautiful that she dug her nails into his shoulders. And he still kept coming. Deeper and deeper, he pressed into her body, filling her so completely that she wasn't sure where her body ended and his began.

"Fi," he groaned, pausing when he was completely inside of her. She tightened her legs around his waist, squeezing him with her inner muscles.

That's when he started thrusting. Fiona had thought that she was finished, that the beautiful climax she'd experience earlier was enough. But as soon as he rolled his hips, she knew that there was more. So much more.

Higher and higher, his body thrust into hers, making her gasp and cry out. It was glorious and she felt her body tremble as she came closer to that glorious pinnacle. When he thrust again, she shattered, clinging to him as he pounded into her core, driving her wild as she writhed under him, her body throbbing with a release that was almost too much, too intense, for her to manage.

When she felt him stiffen against her, she almost cried out with relief and disappointment. Then he collapsed against her, his warm breath caressing her neck and she shivered, intoxicated by the way his body warmed hers, protected hers. It was...the most beautiful experience of her entire life.

"Thank ye," she whispered, feeling a tear slide down her cheek. She closed her eyes, tightening her arms around him.

A long time later, she felt him pull away. A cold breeze made her shiver, so Callum pulled the blankets up around her, tucking her into his bed while he stepped into the bathroom to clean up. Fiona curled up, wondering sleepily if she should get out of the bed and walk home. Tonight had been...better than anything she could have imagined. But she didn't want to overstay her welcome.

That question was answered when Callum came back to bed, sliding in beside her. He pulled her closer, spooning her body against his. And she fell asleep. Just as the darkness took over her conscious thoughts, she might have whispered, "I love you," but she was too tired to worry about it. And she only dreamt it anyway.

Chapter 7

Fiona sighed and snuggled deeper into the delicious warmth. Smiling, she felt Callum's arm tighten around her waist. "Finally," he grumbled, and nipped the lobe of her ear, drawing a sleepy giggle from her.

A giggle? Fiona hadn't ever had a chance to giggle in her life! Giggling implied being carefree and young. She'd never been young. Because of her mother's illness and her father's irresponsibility, her life had been one challenge after another.

When he nuzzled her neck, that sound came again. Another giggle! How outrageous!

But it was a fine morning and Fiona didn't want to analyze anything too deeply. Not right now. She'd go over her actions of last night and, hopefully, this morning, later. When she was alone, she could berate herself for avoiding her responsibilities. But right now, she was going to enjoy being in Callum's arms.

"Bonny bed," she muttered, turning to beam up at him.

Callum's grumbling laughter warned her that he wasn't in the mood to discuss furniture. Thank goodness!

"Nice body," he countered, pulling back slightly so he could better admire her breasts, the soft pink nipples already peaked, as if begging for his attention.

He shifted so his erection was cradled against her stomach, then moved even lower. She gasped as that throbbing member teased her core. But then his mouth covered a nipple and the newest teasing was even more important to pay attention to.

"Dinna ye ever get sore?"

He stopped immediately and lifted his head, his dark eyes looking at her intently. "Are *you* sore?"

Startled at the abrupt cessation of the delicious sensations, her eyes popped open. "Nay!"

His shoulders relaxed slightly, and his hand moved lower, cupping her core. "Would ye tell me if you were?"

She grabbed his wrist, trying to pull his hand away. "Callum, I dinna..." Her words melted into a sensual moan as Callum slipped a finger into her heat and her body seemed to melt, her hips rolling against that finger as it teased and...dear heaven! What was he doing now?

Gasping, she jerked again, her fingers tightening around his wrist, but she wasn't sure if she was trying to pull his hand away or keep it close.

"Ah, I found it," he commented lightly, his features tightening as his desire increased.

Shifting her hips, Fiona grabbed his shoulders, not sure what he was doing, but it felt incredible! "Dinna...stop!" she gasped. And moments later, her body sparkled into a climax that was so intense, her eyes closed and her body clenched around his fingers. She screamed his name, or maybe she just screamed. Fiona wasn't aware of anything other than the intense beauty of what he'd just given her. It was incredible, mind blowing! It was...she breathed out and opened her eyes to find him staring, his hand pressed against her stomach.

"Tha' was amazing," he grumbled. Then shifted so he was poised over her. "Think ye can do it again?"

She shook her head, but her fingers tightened, gripping his shoulders as he rolled a condom down over his shaft. Moments later, he thrust himself into her, pressing deeper and deeper. Fiona shifted, her legs coming up to wrap around his waist and she arched her back, taking him as deeply as she could.

Callum moved slowly at first. But as soon as the friction started, they urged each other on, their bodies tightening, climbing towards that peak. Faster and faster, he thrust into her. He could see that she was struggling and pulled back, gritting his teeth as he moved his thumb over that nub. It only took a few minutes before he felt her body tightening, and he released his control, thrusting harder now, bringing them to that shuddering, shivering climax together.

When it was all over, he rolled to his side, pulling her with him, their breathing labored with the effort to pull as much oxygen into their lungs as possible.

"Nay! No more!" she laughed, but pressed a kiss to his bare shoulder.

He laughed with her, pulling her on top of him. "I'll hold off." His hands stroked her back. "Fer now."

She laughed, pressing her face against his chest. She bit him in reply so he swatted her bottom.

They lay like that for a long time and Fiona wondered why she'd never ventured into the sexual world since college. Then she felt him move and smiled, answering her own question; because she hadn't met Callum yet.

Cautioning her tender heart, reminding herself that this relationship was only temporary, she sat up. "I need a shower."

Carefully extracting herself from his limbs as well as the sheets, she grabbed the blue shirt he'd worn the other day, covering herself as she walked into the bathroom. She flipped on the shower and borrowed his tooth brush to clean her teeth while waiting for the hot water to make its way through the pipes. The cottage was well decorated and well maintained, but she knew that the plumbing in these old houses would take some time.

She watched in the mirror as Callum stepped into the bathroom, growling when he realized that she was using his toothbrush. "Thief," he growled, then swatted her bottom and took a swig of mouthwash. When she finished brushing her teeth, she handed him the toothbrush, winking at him for her audacity.

Callum took the toothbrush, feeling a stab of something odd in his chest at the thought that she felt comfortable enough to use it. Weren't women all obsessed about having their own toothbrush? That hadn't ever made sense to him.

As he brushed his teeth, he watched her slip into the shower and soap up those delectable curves that he'd explored last night. He remembered when his hand had accidentally brushed the back of her knee and she'd gasped. So he'd "accidentally" kept doing it. Then there was that place on her hip. It wasn't ticklish, but he'd nipped it last night at some point and there was a small mark there from where he'd sucked the skin to "make the spot feel better". He liked that. He'd marked her in some small way. She probably had no idea that the hickey was there, but he knew. And it turned him on. It was almost as if she was now his woman because he'd marked her.

And he definitely liked that idea!

Chapter 8

"Coffee," Callum growled, stepping up behind Fiona and putting his hands on her hips. "Why havna ye made me coffee yet, woman?"

She laughed and shrugged. "Ye dinna have any tea, mister. Where's the tea?"

He sighed heavily even as he leaned forward, nibbling at the nape of her neck. "I'm sorry, Fi. I should have gone to the store te get some tea. Especially since I'd been planning a night like last night since the first moment Ah saw ye."

"Is that so?" she asked, doubting the sincerity in his voice even as she smiled at the idea.

"Absolutely! Ye were standing in the sunshine, chatting with yer flowers."

She laughed, remembering. "Is this ye're way of distracting me from getting' me tea?"

He chuckled and turned her around. "How aboot if we head into the village and grab a cup o' something at the coffee shop, then we'll hit the grocery store for more food?"

"I have te work today, remember?"

"It's Saturday. Why would ye work on a Saturday?"

She blinked owlishly. "It is?"

"Aye." He brushed her lips with his. "Let's play hooky and go fer a hike, bring some sandwiches and ye can show me yer favorite native flowers."

She leaned her head back, resting her hands on his chest. "Ye like to hike?"

"I love it. There's a place near my home where I can get away, outside o' the city. It's about an hour's drive, then a long walk up the side of a mountain. But once I reach the top, I can see for miles. It completely clears me mind, reminds me tha' the world is bigger than the problems waiting for me at the office."

She lifted up onto her toes and kissed him. "Tha's exactly how I feel every spring when I watch me flowers pop up out o' the ground. The miracle of life continues on, despite e'erything covering me desk o' the long list of email messages that need answers."

Callum deepened the kiss, his hands starting to roam. She laughed and grabbed his hands. "No' a chance, mister," she warned, but she didn't pull away.

Callum's smile was unrepentant as he grabbed his keys, laced his fingers with hers, and led her out of the house.

As soon as they stepped into the coffee shop, the scents of coffee and chocolate washed over them. It was later than normal, since he'd kept her awake for more than half the night. But there were a good number of people sipping coffee and reading the news, and almost everyone had a baked treat as well. It was hard to ignore the smell of freshly baked bread, especially on a crisp, Saturday morning! There were some treats one just couldn't ignore and fresh baked bread ranked high up on that list.

Fiona and Callum took their drinks over to a small table in the corner and set the plate of four muffins in the center. She'd protested getting four muffins until she'd looked up at Callum, remembering the packed muscles all over his body. And she did mean ALL over his body. Even his calves and thighs were hard muscled and fascinating!

He cut the muffins in half, then quickly devoured three of those halves. They talked politics and the latest news about happenings around the world. Since she lived in Europe and he lived in the States, it was a fascinating conversation about perspectives, the contrasting opinions based off their differences. Fiona noticed that his brogue faded when he thought about his home in the US, but intensified when they discussed any issue here in the village. She knew that the changes in accent intensity, unless it was faked, was due to a person's ability to empathize. Another mark in Callum's side!

After about an hour, Fiona looked around and sighed.

"What's wrong?" he asked, instantly alert.

She tilted her head, her eyes darting around the room. "I usually dinna come te this place."

"Why not? The coffee is excellent and these muffins are my new forever favorite."

Fiona smiled, in complete agreement about the muffins.

"I dinna stop by here because I canna just sit and relax."

Callum looked around, uncomprehendingly. "Everyone else seems to be doing so."

"Aye, but when I try, I'm usually interrupted. People..." she paused, grimacing. "I shouldna be so irritated, but normally, someone, or several someones, pops over to me table and asks me te help them with their business idea or give advice on marketing or accounting or whate'er problem they are having."

He nodded knowingly. "When I came by here several days ago, I overheard a couple people debating a business issue. They all agreed they would discuss it with you."

Her shoulders slumped. "Ah feel as if I should help them all in whate'er way they need. But I'd definitely appreciate better boundaries."

"Have ye e'er left the village? Gone on a trip for a few weeks?"

Her eyes lit up at the suggestion, but she shook her head. "Nay. I worry tha' leaving would cause a panic."

He reached over and took her hand. "I think it's time for ye to let yer baby business members do a bit of their own research. Let them sink or swim. Ye dinna need te be the savior te e'eryone who works 'round here."

She listened and considered his words. "No one helped them afore. And the village almost died out. Now, tourists come here. The small businesses are thriving, they've developed an online presence, and they ship their goods all o'er the world." She smiled with pride. "Our little town has become competitive."

"Aye, but at what price te yer personal freedom? Yer privacy?"

She sighed and nodded. "It's become a burden lately, but I canna seem te get them te understand that I canna be available te them all the time."

He winked at her as he stood up. "Ah'll help ye. And we'll start by going on that hike ye promised me."

She smiled and stood up, in full agreement of the hike. They stopped by the grocery store, stocking up on picnic items. It only took about twenty minutes to reach the trailhead and then they walked up the side of the craggy hill. It was a long hike, but not especially difficult except for a few places that required a bit of climbing over boulders. It was worth reaching the top and settled down for their lunch. The view was breathtaking!

Where the hell was she? It was three o'clock in the afternoon. Fiona should be outside, working in her garden by now. He'd been sitting in this cold, prickly spot for hours! He'd gotten here well before she normally took a break, just so that he wouldn't be noticed. So why wasn't she here?

He remembered her driving the wrong way on the road the other day and then last night, she'd organized that damn poker party. Fiona wasn't maintaining her usual routines and it was really pissing him off! How was he supposed to kill her if she was acting so unpredictably?

He chuckled at that thought, wondering what a therapist would say.

Sighing, he twirled the syringe in his fingers, watching as the needle pointed upwards one moment, then spinning it again and seeing that it pointed downwards this time.

Vaguely, he wondered what would happen if he injected the contents of the syringe into his own leg. Would he feel light headed? Would he enjoy the sensation? Probably. He'd done drugs in his youth. Nothing crazy, like heroine or meth. But he'd certainly enjoyed a joint or two. And cocaine? Yeah, that had been a serious rush. Too bad he hadn't been able to maintain an income that would allow for a coke habit. That high had been mind-bending!

Alas, the one time he'd stolen a car, the damn thing had a tracking device. The police had nabbed him easily that time. Blasted technology! And because of that arrest, his fingerprints were on file now. The couple a few years later...well, he'd had to dispose of their bodies and it had been just a bit of bad luck that he'd taken the car and gotten caught. He'd hidden the knife in what he'd *thought* was an abandoned castle. Now the knife was in there somewhere, a threat to his freedom. A loose end that he needed to eliminate.

Hence, why he needed Fiona out of the castle so he could search the damn place!

Yes, he needed Fiona gone.

So if he did nothing else during his time in this godforsaken village, he had to find that damn knife! And since the knife was hidden in a box that was somewhere in the castle...!

Fiona had to go!

Chapter 9

"Who was that?" Fiona asked, watching with a smile as he tucked his cell phone back into his pocket. He looked like a cat who had discovered a vat of cream.

"Me friends are on their way. They've decided that Kasim will be the last to arrive. He'll be the cream o' the crop o' people yer father will want to play poker with."

She laughed, nodding her head. "Ye're right. There's no way he'll be able to resist playing with the Sheik of Alistar." She twirled in her office chair, standing up and coming around to the other side of her desk. "But seriously, I think Marco Hudson will also be an excellent lure as well. Me father actually had a meeting wi' him several years ago. I have about twenty thousand shares o' stock in his company. He's good. Very good!"

Callum grabbed her hand and pulled her onto his lap. "No' as good as I am," he growled, lowering his head to nibble at her neck.

"Hello?"

A voice called out from the first floor.

Fiona froze, looking into Callum's eyes. "Who is that?"

"And why the hell didn't he knock?" he demanded. Furious, he stood up and took her hand in his. "Yer father is still in the next village, aye?"

She shrugged and followed him down the winding stone stairs. "He said he wouldna be back until later tonight. That's why I thought it would be okay to work here again today instead o' at your rental cottage."

Callum glared at the doorway that would lead to the ancient, stone stairway. "So, who the hell thought he could just walk into yer house? Does tha' happen often?"

"Except for my father, who actually owns the castle, no one has e'er just walked in without knocking first," she replied, hurrying down the stairs behind him. "I wonder why a burglar would announce himself first, though!"

They stepped into the main area, but no one was there. A sound from the living room caught their attention and Callum stepped in front of Fiona. "I dinna suppose ye'd go back upstairs and let me handle this, would ye?"

She shot him a withering look and he nodded. "That's wha' I thought."

They moved silently down the stairs, stepping into the grand foyer together. But no one was around.

Another noise came from the living room and Fiona moved towards the doorway.

"Father Finn?"

The man whipped around, a guilty expression on his face that he quickly hid behind an engaging smile. "Eh, lass! I was hoping to catch ye!" He walked towards her, jerking his black, clergy jacket back into place.

Fiona glanced behind him, wondering why he'd been standing in front of the sideboard, opening the drawers. What was he looking for? Surely he wasn't trying to steal the silver? She didn't actually own any silver. She'd learned long ago not to buy anything that her father could sneak out of the house and sell.

"Were ye searching through me flatware, Father?" she asked, suspicion lacing her voice.

The man actually managed to look hurt. He glanced behind him, then back at Fiona and shook his head. "Nay, lass," he replied. "I was puttin' some stuff away! I found a few knives sitting on the foyer table and I ken how ye like things neat, eh? I don't ken how the knives were out there. Seems like an odd place te leave yer utensils."

Fiona looked back at the foyer table, doubting herself now. Had her father tried to steal her utensils, and changed his mind when he realized nothing was sterling silver? It was certainly possible.

Blinking, she tried to shake off her suspicions. This was the village priest! He'd only been in town for a few months, but during that time, he'd done a wonderful job. His sermons were lively and engaging, and he worked hard to visit the parishioners during the week. He'd even suggested starting a church day care, to help out the parents with small children.

She'd always thought Father Finn was a good man. However, Fiona couldn't shake the sensation that he was lying. A priest, *lying*? Didn't that violate...well, a lot of church rules? And how in the world had he gotten inside? She'd locked the front door. Hadn't she?

No, she must have left it open. However, since Fiona lived alone except for her father's sporadic visits, Fiona had gotten into the habit of locking the doors, even when she was outside, carrying a key just because the castle was so big and she couldn't see all of the entrances. Many people in the village left their doors open, but she never had.

Pulling herself back to the present, she folded her hands in front of her. "How can I help ye, Father?"

The man's smile widened. "Well, I was wonderin' if ye might have time for a wee chat aboot a special project I'd like te start."

Fiona's head tilted. "A new project? What kind o' project?"

"Aye, the church needs a new roof. And I'd like to rally the villagers to get a fundraising committee going. I donna want te go te the bishop for the funds fer the new roof. No' until we try and raise the money ourselves, ye ken?"

"Aye," she replied, nodding her head, but she was still suspicious. Now that she'd caught the man sifting through her dining room drawers, she wondered if this fundraising effort was...something more? But what?

Father Finn continued, oblivious to her suspicions. "So, I was wonderin if ye might have a mind te head up that committee. Ifn' ye think it might be a worthwhile effort?"

She felt Callum's presence behind her. The strength of his presence soothed her. She wasn't crazy, she told herself. This man, Father Finn, had been looking through her drawers. She'd always listened to her instincts when it came to making business decisions. Why was she hesitating right now?

Callum's warmth behind her strengthened her and she straightened her shoulders. Smiling politely, she explained, "Ah think that's a grand idea, Father. Howe'er, we're havin' another poker night tonight, so I'm gonna have te talk to ye aboot the committee maybe next week. And later, some of Callum's friends are flying in from out of town te join in the fun." She paused. Her instincts were still screaming that something wasn't right. "Would ye like te join us again, Father? The money will be higher, but yer a grand poker player. Ye won a good deal of money from some of the people last night. And the people coming into the village soon will have deeper pockets. Perhaps ye could get a good start on that roof replacement money from these people." She grinned, finding the idea more appealing than she'd anticipated. "Ye wouldna have te hold back, like I know ye were the other night. Being a priest and a godly man, I know ye didna want te fleece the villagers. I was doin' the same."

Father Finn puffed up like a puffer fish, his eyes lighting at the offer. His need to feel important and special only reinforced her opinion that something was definitely off. Something that she hadn't sensed until now.

"What's the buy in fer this special game?"

Fiona waved that question away. "Oh, there's no specific buy in, Father." She felt Callum's hand on her shoulder. Apparently, Father Finn noticed as well because his eyes narrowed on Callum's hand, but he pulled his gaze quickly up to hers again. Another red flag, she thought. "Just bring whatever money ye have on ye. But the play will be a bit steeper."

"Who would these friends be, lass?" He looked at Callum.

His hand tightened on her shoulder so Fiona let him answer. "Marco Hudson, and his wife, Chloe, are flying in this morning. And," he paused to look at Fiona.

Callum was about to say something more, but Father Finn interrupted by saying, "*The* Marco Hudson? I've read stories about him. He shifted all of his import-export business down from some port in the northern states to a port in South Carolina, right? Wasn't there a big kerfuffle in the shipping industry o'er it?"

Callum nodded. "Aye. The very same Marco Hudson. He did that o'er a year ago."

Father Finn's hands clapped together. "Ah'm honored that ye think I am good enough te play with Mr. Hudson."

Callum grinned. "It's actually his wife, Chloe, that ye'll need te watch out fer."

"Is that so?"

"Also, Angela Bertuccio an' her husband, James Rutherford, will be here."

Father Finn's jaw went slack and for a long moment, Fiona wondered if he'd back out. Why did the mention of those two make him wary?

"Well, that's very generous of ye te let me play with the big guns tonight!" He laughed and clapped his hands together. "I'll just get oot o' yer way, lass."

The man rushed out of the dining room and almost slammed the front door closed in his hurry to get on his way.

Fiona turned, lifting confused eyes up to Callum. "Was that odd o' am I just...?"

"That was definitely odd," Callum agreed.

"And was he...?"

"Trying te steal from ye?" Callum finished when she hesitated. "Aye. I think he was."

Fiona smiled, sliding her hands higher along his chest. "I hear more of ye're brogue coming out. It's verra nice."

He looked down at her with cynicism, but he wrapped his arms around her waist, pulling her in closer. "Do ye, now?"

"Aye," she teased. "When do ye're friends arrive?"

He lifted his arm to glance at his watch. "We have a bit of time." His arm went back around her waist. "What did ye have in mind?"

Her grin widened. "Well..."

His laugh was deep and sexy. But a moment later, he glanced over her shoulder at the dining room table. He started backing her up and, initially, his intent wasn't clear. But as soon as she realized what he was thinking, she laughed and shifted, trying to pull away. "Nay!" She wiggled to the side, but Callum easily caught her and pulled her back against his chest. "NO, Callum, ye're no' gonna make love te me on the dining room table."

He chuckled evilly and lifted her up, then slipped between her legs. "Ye think no'?"

"Nay!" But she couldn't stop the laughter when his hands slipped underneath her sweater. Unfortunately, she'd donned clothes that were too easy for him to take off. Or leave on and take advantage of! Her sweater buttoned up the front, which he made short work of, revealing her pretty, black lace bra.

When his mouth covered a taut nipple through the lace, she moaned, no longer fighting him. In fact, her fingers dug into his shoulders, keeping his mouth in place as he drove her wild with that mouth. And his teeth! Good grief, she loved it when he did that thing with his teeth, then soothed her aroused nipple with his tongue. Even a feather-light kiss at the tip made her shiver and whimper for more. For the other side, he pulled the lace away and performed the same actions while he continued to tease and torture the first breast.

Her legs moved higher and she felt his free hand wrap around her waist, then slide lower. A moment later, her body was jerked to the edge of the table. Fiona yelped, her breath coming in gasps of delight and whimpers of need.

Fiona let her hands roam over his chest. She fumbled with his belt, then unzipped his slacks. She heard a muffled groan when she pushed his boxers down, freeing his erection. She wrapped her fingers around his shaft, but she could barely think when he was doing that thing to her breasts and he knew it.

"Condom!" she whispered harshly, wiggling closer to that tempting part of him.

He growled and pulled back. Reaching into his pocket, he pulled out a condom, took her hand and slapped the condom into it. "You do it. I'm busy."

Frantic now, Fiona tore the condom wrapper open with her teeth, tossing it aside before rolling the condom down into place. When it was finally secure, she wrapped her legs around his waist and pulled him closer.

When he pressed into her, she moaned with relief. Unfortunately, her relief was short lived. He shifted, lifting her hips slightly and, she didn't understand how, but with every thrust, the friction against that nub was just perfect! Or maybe it was the fact that he was moving fast! If she'd had enough brainpower to think, she might have smiled at the fact that he was just as frantic as she was. But that wasn't the case.

So when her body exploded sooner than she'd anticipated, it surprised them both. Thankfully, Callum held on, keeping her safe as he followed her into that beautiful oblivion.

When she opened her eyes again, it was to see the ceiling of her dining room. Looking around, she realized that she was draped across the table, Callum still inside of her and kissing her chest softly. The kisses weren't sexually charged. They were soothing, as if he needed to touch her, to kiss her and continue to be one with her.

"Callum," she whispered, her voice quivering with emotion.

He looked up at her and nodded. "I know," he replied, his tone serious and the look in his eyes told her that he felt it too. His arms tightened around her and she held on, her body quaking for a completely different reason this time.

They remained like that for a long moment, holding onto each other as they slowly came back to earth.

Callum held onto Fiona until she stopped trembling. And even after that, he continued to hold her just because he liked it. He loved holding her. It was one of the best parts of sex.

Okay, not the *best* part, he corrected. But it was a heady second place.

Running his fingers down her back, he reveled in the softness of her skin. She was so pale, everywhere! He loved touching her and guessed that he'd always be amazed at the softness of her skin. She was so delicate and yet, so strong. Fiona was strong and capable, but when he held her like this, or more specifically, when she held him like this, he felt powerful and strong. Balanced. He felt like he could conquer the world.

And yet, he needed to talk to her. He knew that this wouldn't be a comfortable conversation. She wasn't going to like it and he didn't want to scare her, but he'd delayed all morning.

The fact that Father Finn was able to get into her home, the castle, which was originally built as a fortress, only made this conversation more urgent.

"Are you okay?" he asked, kissing her bare shoulder as he lifted her higher so that she was sitting on the table once more.

"Aye. More than okay." She smiled and his heart did that odd thumping thing again. Damn, she had to stop smiling at him like that.

No, he never wanted her to stop smiling like that. She hadn't smiled enough in her life. He wanted to make sure that she smiled every damn day for the rest of her life!

They moved into the small bathroom off the main living room, what had most likely been a storage room for armory or perhaps a space to contain the hounds during meals when the castle was first built. Fiona had converted the space into a cozy sitting room, with overstuffed chairs and ottomans, soft lighting, and tables next to the chairs for coffee cups or brandy glasses.

Nothing in the castle was expensive, and he now knew why.

When they were both dressed, he took her hand and led her into the small sitting room. He urged her to sit in the chair while he sat on the ottoman in front of her. He took her hand, holding it in front of her.

"I know ye dinna want to think someone is trying te kill you, but..." he paused and opened his palm to show her the syringe he'd found earlier this morning. He'd put it in a drawer to hide it from her until he could figure out what it was.

"Why do ye have a syringe?" she asked, her hazel eyes wide with confusion and a touch of fear.

"Ah found it this mornin' when I came back from me run. It was on the ground behind a stone wall near the road. I think tha' someone was waiting for ye te walk home last night and, when ye didna return this way, they left, unaware o' the lost syringe."

She shook her head, denying its use. "Nay. That could be just a syringe tha' a diabetic dropped. Or maybe someone was shootin' up and..."

"It's not heroin, nor is it insulin, Fi," he argued. "Remember when I left for an hour while ye were on the phone with your contact in Germany this mornin'?" He waited for her nod before continuing. "Well, I went to the pharmacy in town. Herbert tested the contents o' the syringe an' told me what was in it."

"Nay." She shook her head again, crossing her arms over her chest. "I donna believe it. Ye're trying to convince me that me father was trying to kill me and I dinna believe you."

"Where was ye're father last night?" Callum asked, and even he could hear a return of his brogue as he tried to gentle the truth.

She blinked, then shook her head.

"He wasna here, was he?"

Her lips pressed together, then she sighed, looking down at her hands folded on her lap. "Nay. I just assumed that he'd gone back te London te stay in the flat there."

"But then he was here this morning for breakfast, wasn't he?"

"Aye."

"Would he travel around like that?"

"Nay," she whispered, trying not to accept the truth. But it was hard to ignore the facts. "My father...might ha' spent the night at a friend's house last night."

"Or, he was waiting for ye te walk home." He reached out to touch her. "I canna be sure tha' the culprit is yer father. But ah think we need to take this threat seriously."

Her lip trembled. "Wha' if it isna me father?"

He nodded. "It's possible that it isna him. But tha' means, someone else is trying to harm ye, love."

She swallowed as another horrible possibility occurred to her. "O' harm someone else who lives around here."

He nodded again. "That's certainly true. But Fi, I..." he paused, looking into her eyes. "Ah donna think I could stand it if someone hurt ye." He took her hands. "Ah think I'm in love with ye."

He heard her gasp, then her eyes softened. "Why?"

He understood her question as well as the reasons behind it. And damn, he wished he didn't. His fingers tightened around her tightly fisted hands. "Ye donna think you're lovable. Ye've had a father who only comes around when he needs something from ye. And the people in the village mainly talk te ye fer yer business expertise." He paused, letting his understanding hang in the air before he continued. "I love ye because ye're brilliant and caring. I love ye because ye're...unique and fascinating. Ye challenge me, Fi. And ye've made my life so much better, just by being by me side."

She drew in a shuddering breath. "Ye should hate me. Ah'm going te own this castle. I'm going te keep your birthright."

His fingers tightened on hers. "Ah've actually discovered something, someone, I want more than this pile of rocks." He opened his mouth to say something more, but a banging on the front door interrupted him. With a glare at the empty door, he sighed, squeezed her hands again and stood up. "Ah'll find out who that is an' get rid o' them. We're no' finished wi' this conversation."

He walked out of the sitting room, leaving Fiona staring at her hands. Gritting his teeth, he wondered how long it would take to get rid of whoever was knocking. He estimated thirty seconds, but was determined to beat that time. Fiona needed him. It wasn't fair to lay all of that on her and then not follow up.

Yanking the door open, he found Bernard standing on the other side of the door adjusting a blue ascot around his neck. It wasn't even a real ascot. It was fake, with a buckle, so that he didn't need to learn how to tie it properly.

"What?" Callum growled.

Bernard jerked around, startled by a male voice when he was obviously expecting Fiona to answer the door.

"Oh...Uh...!"

"I donna have time fer this!" Callum snapped, unwilling to be patient after what he'd overheard after the poker night. The man assumed Fiona would eventually submit to him, despite Fi's continuous rejection. He was obtuse, as well as ignorant and insensitive.

Bernard jerked to attention, but stammered slightly.

Out of the corner of his eye, Callum watched an SUV pull into the castle parking lot and park next to Bernard's ten year old Land Rover. Callum kept his attention on Bernard, but relaxed as he watched Marco, Chloe, Dash, and Maxine step out of the vehicle. A second vehicle followed. He suspected Angela and James were in that vehicle.

He was wrong. The six of them were all here, but Josh and Marnie, Maxine's younger sister, stepped out of the second vehicle. Josh was a damn good lawyer and Marnie was a law student. Josh and Angela occasionally worked on cases together and they were a scary good team. As soon as Marnie graduated from law school next year, she would join Josh and...well, the legal profession should be shaking in their shoes with the three of them collaborating on cases.

Focusing on the dunce in front of him, he waited for Bernard to get to the point.

"I want in!" the man blurted out.

Callum saw the others walking towards the front door, most of them admiring the impressive castle. Some of them were focused on the rotund man at the front door.

"No."

Bernard sighed, shaking his head. "I don't mean about right now. I want in on the poker game tonight."

Callum groaned silently. "No."

The man's chest expanded but instead of looking intimidating, he looked like an irate puffer fish. "Why not? I'm an excellent player!"

"The stakes are much higher tonight. Ye canna afford this game."

The man wheezed in pathetic indignation. "I can well afford it, no matter the stakes. I have a *very* sizeable inheritance and, as one of the wealthiest members of this community, I demand to be a part of the festivities tonight!"

The man's Scottish accent was non-existent now. He had a bit of a Manchester sound to his words now.

"I don't mind if he wants to play," someone said behind him.

Callum glanced at Marco who had a predatory grin on his face. The man towered over his wife, but even she looked as if she wanted to take Bernard down several pegs. Angela...God help Bernard because Angela looked ready to roast him on a spit.

Callum brought his attention back to Bernard. "Fine. Ye're in. Bring your money a' six o'clock. Here, no' the pub. See if ye can keep up. Now get out of the way so that me friends can come inside." Callum stepped to the side and everyone who had been patiently standing behind Bernard gathered around him, hugging Callum and ignoring the little cockroach. When all of his friends were inside, Callum slammed the door shut behind him, unconcerned with Bernard's startled look.

"Good to see you all," he called to the group that was now gazing in awe at the ancient foyer.

"This was really an old castle?"

"It still is," a female voice called out.

Everyone turned as Fiona stepped out of the drawing room. She smiled at Callum and, apparently, her anxiety over their conversation was gone. In her eyes, he only saw confidence and...damn, his breath caught in his throat. Love. The love she felt for him was shining clearly through those beautiful, hazel eyes.

He reached for her and she took his hand, then leaned against his side, wrapping his arm around her waist as he said to the group, "And this is the amazing woman who restored this pile o' stones to its former glory." He made the introductions, everyone greeting Fiona warmly. Fiona was part of his "family" now and they all accepted her as one of their own. It was how they worked. They had all, every person in this room as well as Kasim and Rosalee, had gone through hell and come out the other side stronger. Fiona perfectly matched that description. Plus, she was the most beautiful woman in the group, in his opinion.

"Why donna we head into the kitchen? I had food delivered earlier in case anyone was hungry. There's fresh beer and wine, as well as sandwich makings."

Everyone sighed with relief, then followed Callum and Fiona into the kitchen.

The next several hours, they sat around Fiona's large dining room table discussing the plan for the night. Everyone was warned to keep an eye and ear open for Duncan's return. But with the whole group strategizing, it was easy to create a more concrete plan, as well as the coup de gras – the night with Kasim and Rosalee – in more detail.

Once the plan was hashed out, there was laughter and teasing all around. They pulled out decks of cards and started playing games. While they were all well versed in the art of poker. This afternoon was just about enjoyment. By four o'clock that afternoon, the entire group was in a vicious, hilarious game of "Mad Solitaire" with hands flying, cards being slapped down on top of hands and cards, accompanied by a lot of laughter and fun.

By the time Duncan showed up, right before five o'clock, the group was having a raucous good time.

"What's going on here?' he called out, his charming façade firmly in place.

Fiona stood up, wiping a tear of laughter from her cheek as she explained, "Father, these are some o' Callum's friends. They arrived for a bit o' a long weekend and we are having another poker night."

Callum turned to introduce Duncan to the group, and Duncan's chest seemed to expand with every new person he identified. "Well, it's a great pleasure to have you here in my humble home." He turned to glare at Fiona. "I'm guessing my daughter hasn't offered any refreshment." He chuckled with a patronizing pat on her shoulder, shaking his head as if he was the only person who knew how to host an evening event. "How about if I pull out my best scotch before we all settle down for that spot of poker, eh?"

His Scottish accent was completely gone, replaced by an upper-class British accent.

Because that was exactly what everyone was hoping for, they all agreed and the dining room table transformed into a poker table.

Around seven o'clock, Bernard showed up. By that point, Duncan was already sweating, trying to mask his nervousness.

"Well, this looks like a delightful evening!" Bernard announced, clapping his hands together as he took the seat that Duncan had just vacated.

Fiona watched, delighted that her father was obviously running short of funds. Everything was working perfectly!

Chapter 10

The next morning, Duncan pulled Callum aside, asking for a private word. "What can I do for you, Duncan?" Callum asked, stepping into the library of the castle.

The previous evening's poker game had wiped out Duncan's available funds. The night had ended early, around ten o'clock, all of his friends making comments about tonight's game, mainly about Kasim and how important he thinks he is. Callum knew what Duncan was about to ask and wanted to rub his hands together.

"About tonight's poker game..."

Callum lifted his hand. "I will completely understand if ye canna make it tonight. Kasim and his wife, Rosalee, will be here and the stakes are going to be e'en higher than they were last night."

Duncan's features paled slightly. "Higher?"

Callum laughed. "Aye, last night, we were just warming up. The last time we played with Kasim, he won all of our money. So tonight, we're oot for revenge."

Duncan shifted on his feet. "Kasim is...?"

"You would know him as the Sheik o' Alstair. But to the rest o' us, he's just Kasim."

The news that royalty would be here seemed to brighten Duncan's mood. Immediately, his eyes morphed from worried to overly confident. Duncan gave his most charming smile and walked over to the liquor cabinet. "I have a proposition for you," he started off, pouring two large portions of scotch into glasses.

"Wha' kind o' a proposition?"

Duncan smiled, then handed Callum a glass.

"I want in on the game tonight again."

Callum took the glass of scotch, but didn't drink it. It was five o'clock in the evening. He generally liked to be coherent when destroying one's enemy. Drinking this much scotch wasn't conducive to brain function. Or liver function, for that matter.

Callum shrugged casually. "Ye played wi' e'eryone last night and, despite yer losses, ye're an excellent poker player. Tonight, ye have a chance te win back yer money. Ye're more than welcome te join in the game. We donna exclude people."

The man smiled, then tilted his head slightly. "Well, that's the thing. I find that I'm a bit short on cash at the moment."

"Lost too much on the game last night?" Callum asked, using what he hoped was a friendly tone.

"Exactly," Duncan replied, chuckling as he peered down at the scotch, twirling the liquid around in the glass. "I wanted to be a good host to your friends, so I let them win some very big hands. They all should be quite flush with cash right about now." Another chuckle and another "charming" smile.

"Trust me, ye dinna have te hold back with me friends." Nor had he. They had beaten him out of his cash easily and fairly. None had even needed Fiona's tips on his "tells". Duncan's facial expressions were pretty obvious. Even now, the man rubbed a finger over his upper lip, letting Callum know that he was bluffing.

"Yes, well, it doesn't matter *why* I lost to your friends last night. I was just...well, I was hoping you'd spot me enough cash to go heavily in tonight. I know I can pay you back after tonight. I have several excellent business adventures that are going to pay off very soon. And since I'm the primary holder of those businesses, I'll be well off after that."

"Wha' businesses?"

Duncan blinked, startled that someone would dare to ask for details. "Excuse me?"

"Wha' are the businesses that are about to come into an influx of cash? And if they are so successful, why wouldn't you reinvest that cash back into the business? That's what a smart business person would do." He glanced out the window where he could see Fiona sitting in the sunshine. The sun was bright today. She needed to move into the shade to protect her skin. "Tha's what Fiona does. Tha's one of the many reasons she's done so well in business."

Duncan's jaw clenched. "Fiona has done well because I tell her where to invest her money. She relies on my business knowledge. Without me, she'd be out on the street."

Callum's eyes narrowed. "She owns her own home," he corrected.

The man's temper snapped. Obviously, Duncan wasn't used to being called out. "This is *my* home! I own MacGreggor Castle!"

Callum's eyebrow lifted, feigning surprise. "Since ye won this castle in a card game with my father, I'm painfully aware o' the fact that ye own MacGreggor Castle." He sighed and lifted his untouched glass of scotch. "I was referring to the flat in London where Fiona sends ye when she wants ye oot o' her hair."

The insult hit the mark. "Now see here!" Duncan started off. "Fiona and I have an agreement."

"O' course ye do," Callum replied, tired of the argument already. He wanted to go outside and...hell, he'd protect Fiona from the sunshine with his own body if need be.

He stood up, intending to do just that. But Duncan must have realized that he was losing control of the argument.

"Wait!" he yelped, standing up as well. There was a slight sheen of sweat on his forehead. He smiled, trying to regain his charm offensive. "Maybe we can make a deal."

"What kind of a deal?" Callum asked. He realized that this was exactly what he'd been working towards. Ever since landing in Scotland, this had been the plan. But now that it was here, all he wanted was to go out and protect Fiona. He wanted to stand by her side and hear her laughter. That was when he realized that getting the castle away from Duncan was much less important than being with Fiona.

Fiona, however, wanted her home. And because he wanted to make Fiona happy, he turned away from the window and the distraction of her beautiful, pale skin, forcing his thoughts back to the conversation. "Wha's the deal?"

"As I said moments ago, I was hoping you could spot me tonight."

Callum went very still. This was it. This was the moment he'd been waiting for. Twenty years of his life, he'd been burning with a need for retribution against this man. He glanced out the window again. Fiona laughed at something Chloe was saying, leaning their heads close together as they talked.

Bringing his gaze back inside, he looked at Duncan. The older man's eyes were too similar to Fiona's. But whereas Fiona's eyes were intelligent and sharp, Duncan's were calculating.

He was going to cheat. Something in Callum's gut warned him that the older man had a plan.

"What's going on?"

Callum turned to find Kasim standing in the doorway with his wife, Rosalee, by his side.

"You old bastard!" Callum laughed, relieved that Kasim was here, safe and sound.

Kasim chuckled and they hugged, genuine affection in their embrace.

When he pulled back, he kept his hand on Kasim's arm. "Ye look great! I guess Rosalee has been keeping ye well stocked in chocolate cupcakes?"

Kasim chuckled and turned to smile down at his wife. The dark haired woman laughed, moving closer as Kasim wrapped an arm around her waist.

There was a bit of commotion as the others moved in from outside, probably to refresh everyone's drinks. Or maybe, they were all heading inside to get ready for the poker game.

But someone, Angela, by the sound of the shriek, realized that Kasim had arrived. Seconds later, a female blur raced by, knocking Callum out of the way as Angela threw herself into Kasim's arms. Kasim laughed, hugging the tiny Italian dynamo affectionately, lifting her clear off her feet. Callum pulled Rosalee out of the way, laughing at the outrageous duo.

"You're here!" Angela gasped, stepping back as Kasim set her down. "You look great! No stress in ruling the world these days?"

"Always stress. But it's not too bad."

Angela turned to smile at Rosalee. Their embrace was a bit less effusive, but no less affectionate. "Is he being good to you? Because if not, you just give me the word and I'll take him down!"

Rosalee laughed, hugging the crazy woman. "Oh, he's horrible! All the time!"

Angela giggled and hugged Rosalee again, ignoring Kasim's warning growl before he pulled Rosalee out of Angela's arms and back against his side. The others laughed and greeted the newcomers with intense affection.

When everyone was done, Callum saw Fiona lingering in the back, obviously intimidated. He beckoned her forward, taking her hand as he pulled her closer. "Kasim, I'd like te introduce ye te Fiona Reid. She's the brains behind this place. She renovated everything, bringing this castle back to life."

Kasim took Fiona's hand, lifting her fingers to his lips in an old-world gesture. "Your efforts are magnificent!"

"Th...thank you!" she whispered, blushing furiously. "It was a labor of love."

Callum chuckled and turned to her father. "Duncan, Fiona's father, wants to join in our poker game tonight."

Everyone turned, their eyes on the man who had been standing back, guzzling scotch, while everyone teased Kasim.

Callum continued, squeezing Fiona to warn her of what's coming next. "He said he has a deal fer me."

Angela stepped forward, her arms crossed over her chest. She feigned a friendly smile, tilting hear head as she said, "Anyone can join in our poker games." Her smile widened then. "After last night's game, you know that we're quite vicious though. The last time Kasim played, what was it? About six months ago since you had time to join us?"

Callum didn't bat an eye at the lie. They'd been at Kasim's palace just over a month ago and she'd won over two thousand dollars. She'd been on a roll that night. Last night, she'd been pretty good too, but Marco had won the most. A roll that Callum was determined to break tonight.

"I brought five thousand for the game tonight,. That, plus the three grand that I won last night puts me in a pretty good position." she announced smugly.

"I'll take that eight thousand with my fifteen thousand," Dash interjected, then winked at her, an evil grin forming on his handsome face.

Angela cocked an eyebrow at him. "Think you're good enough?"

Dash chuckled. "I'll admit that you were on a streak last night. But remember last August?"

Angela glanced at James and her cheeks turned red from whatever memory flashed through her mind. She shuffled her feet as James chuckled. "I was...distracted that time." She shot a glare at her husband before smiling sweetly at Duncan. "But absolutely, you can join our game again."

Duncan's smile brightened as well, but not with triumph. Nope, this smile was his "I'm going to charm you" smile and it sickened Fiona. She'd been the victim of that smile too many times over the years.

"Well, that's the thing. I've been trying to help out the villagers over the past few months, ye see." He glanced around, his eyes halting on Callum since he'd mentioned his soon-to-be profitable businesses as proof of his ability to repay his debts. "As I said, I was hoping someone could spot me a bit just to get me started."

Fiona held her breath, trying to hide her reaction. He was playing right into their hands, so to speak. She didn't look at Callum, terrified she might give their plans away. Her father was a cheat and a liar, but he wasn't stupid and he had powerful instincts about people. If he suspected a trap, then he'd back away. Last night, he'd thought he could win by his brains and charm. Tonight, he would definitely cheat his way to triumph.

Fionna stepped forward. "Ye dinna have anything to put up as collateral fer a loan, Father."

His eyes flashed at her words, but he rallied. "This dinna have te be anything official, love," he mocked. "I'm just asking for a bit of blunt to cover me until I," he glanced around briefly, "fleece your friends, darling."

Angela coughed and stepped forward. "Well, you see, Duncan," she started off in her best lawyer's voice. Trial lawyers were excellent actors and Angela didn't disappoint. "The reason we've all been friends for so long," she paused to wave her arm around, encompassing everyone except him, "is that we've kept things like money and financial issues clean and tidy. If one of us borrows money," she looked around again, "we keep it all legal. I don't mind loaning you some money, but you've got to sign an agreement for that loan."

Duncan's smile faltered. "Are ye kidding me, lass?" Startled, his brogue slipped in again.

Josh stepped forward, fully on board with the situation. "I could draw up an agreement in a few minutes," he offered innocently.

Angela smiled up at him. "You think I can't draw up an agreement?"

The two lawyers chuckled, competition sparking between them. "I think you're fully capable of drawing up an airtight agreement. But let's go with the 'doctor heal thyself' issue, eh?"

She turned and faced him, just as they'd done so many times. "You're right. If I'm going to loan him money, then..."

"It doesna matter," Fiona interrupted, right on cue. "He doesna have collateral." She turned to Duncan. "Ah'm sorry, Father, but they dinna offer loans without collateral. I hope ye understand. It's a business issue." She smiled brightly. "Ye could sit with us though! Our games can get pretty lively!"

"I have a freaking castle as collateral," he snarled, his arms crossing over his chest. "I'll put up the castle and my flat in London as collateral."

Fiona shook her head, one finger raised in protest. "Actually, *I* own the flat in London, Father. Ye dinna have the legal authority to use it as collateral." She gave him a faux-apologetic smile and stepped back. Callum wrapped his arm around her, pulling her close again. They'd all agreed that she'd stay out of the negotiations, just to keep her father from suspecting anything.

"Fine!" he growled, then realized how his anger was coming across to the very people he wanted to impress. "Because I've been so generous lately, and find myself short of cash at the moment, I will be more than happy to sign an agreement to put my home up as collateral for the loan."

Angela's smile brightened. "Perfect!" She turned to her new client. "Would you like to discuss the terms of the loan before we set them down on paper, Duncan?" Angela offered.

Duncan looked around. It was just Angela and Fiona in the dining room now, with Duncan standing by the window. At Angela's question, he turned, his charming smile back in place.

"If my Fiona trusts ye, then I have faith that the terms are fair." They were nice words, but Fiona could see the writhing fury in his eyes. Her father was insulted and embarrassed. He'd never had to sign a legal document before. Good grief, she doubted he even paid taxes! Of course, he had no income, so it wasn't as if he needed to pay income tax. And he didn't bother to pay the property taxes on the castle, leaving that up to Fiona.

Angela shook her head. "I really think that you should go over the terms, Duncan." She called for Josh, who appeared, a cookie in one hand and a soda in the other. "What's up?"

"Could you act as Duncan's lawyer? He should know what he's signing."

He nodded, popped the cookie in his mouth, set the soda on the table, then took the offered papers. "Get gone, ladies!" he announced to Fiona and Angela, waving them off. "I have to confer with my client." He added a wink to Duncan, who literally melted with joy that he had someone on his side. Duncan also loved the fact that the women were kicked out of the room. He genuinely loved his male superiority.

Little did he know that he'd engaged the wrath of one of the best attorneys to ever enter a courtroom.

Fiona walked alongside Angela, so anxious that she felt a bit sick to her stomach.

"Don't worry, Fiona," Angela assured her, putting a gentle hand to her shoulder. "I'm good," she whispered. "More than good." She paused to glance back at the sitting room, the door now closed. When she turned back at Fiona, she continued quietly, "The terms are air tight. He is definitely going to try to wiggle out of the agreement, but I anticipated that. For every battle he wages to fight the terms of the agreement, if he loses, then he incurs legal fees. If he doesn't vacate the premises, both the castle and your London flat within thirty days of the agreement, he incurs your legal fees. The terms are hard to argue. There's no wiggle room. I've fought against some of the slimiest, most wiggle-worthy opponents. Trust me, your father is small time, compared to some of the people I've beaten over the years." She grinned mischievously. "And as your lawyer, I can guarantee that I'm *very* expensive, plus, I've included my hourly rate in the contract. A rate that he must agree to if he signs that document. So he's also agreeing to pay my legal fees."

Fiona laughed and tried to relax. She looked around at the room, loving every small detail she'd lovingly put into the décor. "This isna just a castle to me," she explained, looking around and running her hand along the stone wall. "It's alive. I've worked so hard to make it into a home. An' every time I've tried to buy it from me father, for its actual market value, he's rejected me offers. Ah've even offered above market value several times."

Angela understood. "From what Callum explained to us, the castle represents your father's status within the community and in the world." She grinned. "And that pride is also the reason that we're here, ready to play poker with him. So in the end, you're going to win your home back and not have to pay a dime."

Fiona tried to hide her hope. "Are ye guys *really* tha' good at poker?"

Angela nodded. "Yeah. We are. We held back last night. He's *that* bad of a poker player, which is why it was so easy for us last night."

Fiona laughed, loving her confidence. "Okay, let's go set up the dining room."

The door to the drawing room opened. Angela and Fiona turned, watching as Josh emerged first, needing to duck slightly to avoid hitting his head on the doorframe. Then her father stepped out. She expected him to be wary, or at least, concerned. But there was an air of absolute confidence about him.

Something was wrong!

"He's agreed to the terms."

Duncan chuckled, tossing Josh a conspiratorial look. "He won't let me sign the blasted document until there are witnesses." He waved Fiona towards the sitting room. "Let's do this. You can witness my signature."

"Actually, it would be better if we got someone outside of the family to witness the document," Josh replied.

Duncan's eyes flashed with momentary irritation, but his smile snapped back into place. Fiona wondered if the others saw those flashes of anger, or if she was the only one because she'd lived with him for so long. One glance at Josh and Angela, and Fiona relaxed. They'd caught it too. She wasn't the only one! The relief she felt was overwhelmingly intense. All the years of being gaslighted by her father were now confirmed.

Angela turned. "I'll get the others. We'll meet in the dining room, get this business out of the way, then we can play poker!" She clapped her hands as she made her way into the kitchen.

Fiona, Josh, and Duncan moved to the dining room, Josh still holding the documents. He laid the contract on the table. There were three sets, all of the same papers. The three of them stood there, silently waiting.

One by one, the others filed into the dining room. The men were all tall and powerfully built. And while the women were shorter, some very short, others less so, they all had powerful personalities. They were beautiful in different ways and all very elegant. By the time everyone was in the dining room, drinks and snacks in hand, the dining room felt full and very alive.

"Okay, we're here to witness the signature of Duncan Reid who is putting Castle MacGreggor up as collateral for a loan. You're all here to witness the signing."

There were a few grunts of approval and Duncan looked painfully embarrassed. He didn't like showing weakness of any kind and being short on cash in such illustrious company was humiliating. These were the people he'd intended to impress!

"Let's just get this over with," he grumbled, all signs of charm gone for the moment.

He signed all three sets of papers with a flourish, then stood up. "It's done! Can we please play poker now?"

Kasim was the first to step forward. "I'll sign as one of the witnesses." He bent down and signed his name on the correct line, then stepped back.

Chloe was next, her elegant demeanor heightened by the sleek blond hair style combined with the soft, blue sweater and matching slacks. She moved to the other side of the table and signed her name, a pretty script that contrasted starkly with Duncan's messy signature and Kasim's bold scrawl.

"I'll sign it as well," Dash announced, stepping forward and signing his name.

In the end, everyone signed the document. There was only a place for two witnesses, but Josh quickly made additional lines for all of the witnesses. The end result was an almost comical set of documents, but the deed was done.

"So, I'm the only one confident enough to put my house up for the game?" Duncan called out mockingly. "Am I the only one who actually knows how to play poker?"

There was a silence for a long moment, then a set of keys landed on top of the papers. They were the keys to Marco's house in Charleston, South Carolina. A second key appeared on the table. And a third. Before long, there were ten keys on the table. Everyone was confident enough to put their house up for the game. Even Kasim had added a card with the address of one of his homes on it.

"Wait a minute!" Josh yelped, fishing a key attached to a Tweety Bird key fob out of the pile. He lifted it, eyeing it for a long moment. Then he turned and glared at Marni, his fiancée.

"What?" she asked, her pert chin jutting upward as she matched his glare with interest.

"This is the key to the apartment over my office," he snapped. "*You* rent the place. From *me*!"

She shrugged and gave him an adorable smile. "It's symbolic. I have confidence in you."

He rolled his eyes, pocketed the keys, and pulled her into his arms. He whispered something in her ear that made her blush and lift her face for a sweet, tender kiss.

"Well, now that it's all settled," Fiona announced, clapping her hands. "Let's play poker!"

A knock on the door barely registered in the raucous shifting of furniture around the room. Fiona opened the door, trying to swallow a groan when she saw Bernard and Father Finn on the doorstep.

"We're here for the game!" Father Finn announced. He waved a wad of cash. "Roof repair seed money!"

Bernard grumbled and pushed past them. "You should be ashamed of yourself, Fiona."

"I should?" she asked, turning to frown questioningly at him. Father Finn stepped in as well, shooting her an apologetic look, lingering by her side as if he hoped to protect her.

"Yes. I was under the impression that this game would take place at the pub, like the last one."

"I was too!" Duncan announced, stepping out of the kitchen with a sandwich in hand. "Why the hell *are* we playing here?"

"Why would we go te the pub?" she asked innocently. "It's Friday night. The pub will be full o' people. They donna want to deal with our poker night again."

Duncan's eyes widened as he peered into the dining room where tables and chairs had been set up. "But…you all played at the pub last time. I thought last night was a fluke. Why change things up now?"

Marco stepped out of the dining room. "Security," he explained. "It's too dangerous for Kasim to be in public."

Fiona suspected that half the fun for her father was for the villagers to see him playing world and corporate leaders. Not being seen meant he didn't get the street cred he clearly desired.

Or was there something more? She watched her father carefully, wondering if he'd done something sneaky at the pub. Maybe installed hidden cameras? Didn't matter, she told herself. They were playing here. Whatever cheating aid he'd installed or organized down at the pub would be pointless now.

Rosalee, Marni, Chloe, and Dash all decided to observe. Rosalee, who loved to bake, moved in and out of the kitchen, bringing delicious desserts and snacks to the sideboard.

With so many people playing, they'd divided into two groups.

For the first hour, Fiona was startled to see that her father won every other hand at his table. It was astonishing! She had no idea how he'd upped his game over last night, but he was playing extremely well.

Her heart plummeted! He was going to win! She'd never have her home!

She turned and peeked over at Callum. He wasn't playing at the same table as her father, but he seemed to be having a good time, joking with his friends. Everyone was included, except Bernard, who had been seated at Callum's table.

That man had started out with a huge stack of poker chips, but more than half was already gone after only the first hour of playing. Father Finn's chips were pretty low as well. With a resigned sigh, she accepted that she would most likely be paying for the church roof herself. Mentally, she calculated the cost of a new roof and set aside the funds. Father Finn was acting oddly, probably because he realized now the players around this table were far more adept than the villagers he'd played with during the previous game at the pub.

Her gaze returned to Callum. He must have sensed her eyes on him, because he looked up, staring right back at her. Her heart thudded and she beamed. He loved her! He really loved her! For years, she'd accepted that her life would be here in the village. She'd anticipated a cold, lonely life because...she'd considered herself unlovable! Oh dear heaven, because her father hadn't every truly loved her, she'd thought that she was unlovable!

But Callum loved her! He truly did! She could see it in the way he looked at her. But it wasn't just his gaze. It was this night, the way he touched her, the way he held her and made love with her...it was everything! He had organized all of this, brought his friends from all over the world to this small village just so that she could win this pile of old stones away from her father, once and for all!

Her heart stuttered as a new realization washed over her. She didn't *need* this castle! She didn't need any of it. All she needed was Callum. When they'd spent time at his rented cottage, she'd felt comfortable, warm, and safe, because she'd been with Callum. It wasn't the home she needed, it was him! It was his love that had made her feel secure!

Callum must have caught the surprise in her eyes because he folded his cards and pushed away from the table.

"I'm oot for the next hand," he announced to the other players and stood up. He walked towards her, his eyes never leaving hers. When he was in front of her, he asked, "Are ye okay?"

She stared up into those dark eyes of his and her heart melted. "Aye," she replied, her lips curling into a wide, happy smile. "Aye, I'm really, truly okay!"

He stroked her cheek and let his hand slide down to cup her throat, giving her the warmth she hadn't even known she needed. "What are ye thinking so hard aboot?"

"I love you!" she whispered, then froze, stunned that she'd admit it aloud when they were surrounded by so many people.

He was just as shocked, but he recovered immediately. He took her hand and led her into the kitchen. Rosalee and Chloe were there, so he growled and led her into the next room. This one was empty and he pulled her into his arms, his lips hovering a centimeter above hers. "Say it again," he ordered.

"I love you!" she whispered, then went up on her toes and kissed him. She kissed him with all of the pent up love she'd so desperately wanted to offer to someone. Her father hadn't wanted or needed her love. He'd rejected it so many times during her lifetime, crushing her dreams and hurting her in so many ways.

But Callum, he wasn't anything like her father. He was the exact opposite of that bastard!

"I love you!" she said again, thrilled to be able to say it to him. "I love ye so much!"

He kissed her again, sending shivers all the way down to her toes. His hands cupped her head, deepening the kiss, causing her head to spin out of control. She leaned into him, loving the way he kissed her.

When he finally lifted his head, he was laughing softly. "Ye chose the worst possible time te tell me that!"

She laughed and hugged him, feeling his arms tighten around her. "Hey, you told me ye loved me only moments before e'eryone arrived yesterday!" He laughed and kissed her neck. She smiled and said, "Ah'm so sorry that it's taken me so long to realize it." She pulled back and looked up at him. "Will ye marry me?"

A startled laugh burst out of him, and he nodded enthusiastically. "Yes! Damn it woman, I'm supposed to ask you to marry *me*!"

She grinned, wiggling against him. "Yeah, well, ye snooze, ye lose!"

He chuckled, then brushed his lips against hers again. "Let's go win yer home away from yer father."

She shook her head. "I don't need the castle," she whispered up to him. "I thought I did. I thought that the castle was me home and me security." She kissed his chin. "But ye've replaced that. I realized that it isna the building that I need, it's you. It doesna matter where I am, you're the person I need by my side. You make me feel comfortable."

He growled. "Ye are definitely not going to feel comfortable tonight!"

Fiona laughed, hugged him again, then said, "Let's go win *your* castle!" she urged.

Callum grinned. "Let's go win *our* castle."

She nodded, and hand in hand, they returned to the dining room.

"She loves me!" he hollered.

No one bothered to even look up. "Duh!" came the reply from Marco. "We all knew that as soon as we saw you two together." He picked up the two replacement cards, adding them into the cards in his other hand.

Bernard looked up, his eyes owlish as he tried to understand what was going on. "Huh?" he prompted. No one clarified anything as Kasim picked up all of the money in the center of their table.

"So, when is the wedding?" Kasim asked, sorting his poker chips into piles

"Aye!" called out Father Finn. "And where's he takin ye on the honeymoon?"

Everyone chuckled, but they were mostly focused on the poker game.

Callum kissed her again. "I have some work te do." A moment later, he sat back down in his chair, picking up and sorting the cards.

Fiona grinned and leaned a shoulder against the wall, watching Callum with love in her gaze.

Rosalee came out with another platter of sandwiches. "Congratulations!" she whispered, giving Fiona a one-armed hug. "I think you should have your wedding at Kasim's seaside cottage. It's absolutely lovely and it would make a magical honeymoon spot as well!"

"It's a perfect place for a honeymoon," Kasim agreed loudly, not looking up as he focused on his hand.

"That's very generous of you," Fiona replied, overwhelmed by the offer. "I just–"

"We accept," Callum called out. He frowned at Fiona. "They stayed at me place in Colorado fer their ski vacation last winter." He turned to glare at Kasim. "About time ye reciprocated, ye cheap bastard."

Everyone laughed because they knew that Kasim was ridiculously generous.

Then the group quieted again until the loudest sound was the clinking poker chips .

Rosalee stepped back into the kitchen, which was her happy place, and Fiona was just about to follow her when a movement out of the corner of her eye caught her attention. There was something odd about her father's coat. Had it always been pulled back like that? She watched for another moment, trying to determine what was off about his clothing. No, it wasn't his coat that was off, it was his tie. Why was he wearing a tie? None of the other men, except for Father Finn, was wearing anything around their neck. Everyone was in shirt sleeves, casually dressed while her father was still wearing his wool sports jacket along with a tie.

She narrowed her gaze at him, cringing when he won another hand.

Standing there, she waited, her suspicions on high alert. She turned, looking pointedly at Dash, trying to send him a silent message. But he was focused on Bernard.

Fiona turned her attention back to her father, watching his hands. Sure enough, she saw the slip of his fingers! He'd just pulled a card out of his sleeve!

"Stop!" she yelled, startling the whole group. She didn't care!

Walking over to her father, she stood over him, daring him to lie to her again. "Take off your jacket!" she ordered.

Duncan looked up at her. The startled terror in his eyes told her that she was right. He was cheating!

"Darling, I'm fine the way I am," he waved her off and turned to the others, laughing indulgently. "Women," he chuckled. "Always trying to manage us."

Dash had come over and was now looming over Duncan. "What's wrong?"

"I just saw me father pull a card oot o' his sleeve." She indicated the large pile in front of him. "Tha's how he's been winning so easily. He's cheating!"

Duncan's jaw dropped, but he rallied quickly. "How dare you!" Duncan roared, leaping to his feet.

Refusing to be intimidated by him any longer, she stepped into his personal space, her eyes narrowing as fury engulfed her. "Take *off* yer coat!" she hissed.

Duncan's face turned a painful looking crimson. "Get the hell out of me house!" he snapped, then started to sit down, already dismissing her. "I want ye gone! Get yer things and get oot of here, tenight!" He settled into his chair and shifted. "I wilna have any daughter o' mine accusing me o' cheating!" Gone was his British accent, telling everyone that he was frazzled.

Fiona's confidence wobbled. Was there a possibility that she'd miss-seen something? She'd been so sure a moment ago. But had she misunderstood?

Dash moved closer. "Why don't you just remove your jacket, Duncan?" he offered, his tone cool and polite. "It's a bit warm in here anyway."

Duncan waved the bigger man away and started to pick up his cards. "I'm fine. Let's get back to the game." His accent wobbled this time.

Fiona gave Dash a pleading look. "I swear to you, I saw him pull something from his sleeve."

Dash nodded and grabbed Duncan's arm. He lifted it higher and peered down into the sleeve, ignoring Duncan's feeble attempts to pull away.

"Let go o' me!" Duncan roared. "This is outrageous! Are ye seriously gonna listen te a mere female? She's oot o' her mind!"

Everyone held their breath as Dash reached into the sleeve of Duncan's jacket and...!

Slowly pulled a card out. He tossed it onto the table. Then reached in and pulled out another one. And a third! He grabbed Duncan's other sleeve and pulled out four more.

"Check his tie," Fiona urged, trembling with anger and embarrassment. Her father was a cheater! He'd cheated her new friends!

Sure enough, there were two other cards hidden in the folds of his tie! How in the world had he managed that?

Callum stood up, bracing his hands on the table as he glared down at the cringing man. "Think ye can beat us *without* cheating?" he snarled.

Duncan's jaw slackened and he looked around at the others warily. "Maybe, I should just..."

"Oh no," Marco replied, leaning lazily back in his chair. "You're not leaving this table. You don't get to cheat us and just walk away." Fiona felt Chloe's hand on her upper arm, squeezing slightly. "We're going to keep playing. And let's just see how good you are without the extra cards to help your hand."

Duncan's face turned bright red and a sheen of sweat formed along his upper lip. "I...I..!"

"Deal!" Kasim ordered, sliding the cards to Callum.

Callum shuffled quickly, and started dealing the cards across the table. No one touched them, not until all the cards were dealt.

Finally, he set the remaining cards in front of him. "The previous chips stay in the pot. Everyone ante up."

Everyone added their chips into the already high pile.

Dash stood behind Duncan, watching carefully, his gaze intent as he watched Duncan's play.

He lost! He lost that hand as well as the next four hands! Callum, Kasim, Marco, and Angela all raised the stakes on each round. Even better, Fiona had confidence that *they* weren't cheating.

Within the next hour, Duncan's pile of chips had diminished to less than half of what he'd had and he was sweating profusely.

"Want to bow out?" Kasim asked wickedly, glancing pointedly at the pile of chips.

"Not a chance!" Duncan hissed, then forced himself to smile. "What's it like being the leader of such a powerful country?" he asked, trying to schmooze "his" guests.

"It has its moments," Kasim replied, then raised again, tossing three thousand dollars' worth of chips into the pile.

"That client ye had last month," he tried again, turning to Angela.

Angela shook her head. "You probably want to focus on the game," she whispered, nodding to him since it was his turn.

He casually tossed the required chips into the pile.

Angela won that hand. Fiona had no idea how much was in that pile, but it was a lot!

Kasim gathered Angela, Callum and Marco with his gaze. "Should we raise the stakes on this next round, then?"

Duncan's features paled, his tongue darting out to nervously lick his lips. "Raise the stakes?"

Angela shrugged casually as she stacked up the poker chips she'd just won. "I mentioned that we are a vicious group of players, Duncan." She sneered delicately. "And we don't have to cheat to win."

Duncan rubbed the back of his neck.

"We won't consider you a coward," Kasim inserted softly, "if you want to back out now." He glanced down at the chips. "You would only owe Angela roughly one hundred thousand pounds if you stopped now."

Marco dealt the cards. "You could get a loan to pay that off and still retain ownership of Castle MacGreggor."

Duncan shifted in his chair, trying to appear casual. But the scent of fear was emanating from him now. "I'm in." He turned and smiled at Kasim. "So, how many other world leaders have you met?"

Kasim picked up his cards, shifting them around in his hand. "Let's play poker. We can discuss world politics later."

Duncan's face fell. Fiona understood exactly what her father was trying to do. Duncan wanted stories that he could share with his drinking buddies later. Stories that would make him the center of attention as he related how he played poker with a sheik.

He turned to Marco. "I have some contacts in London tha' might benefit yer business. I've heard that ye are into importing and exporting goods from all o'er the world."

"Ante up," Marco replied flatly, his eyes hard and uncompromising.

Duncan tossed his opening bid chips into the center of the table.

Everyone exchanged cards and Fiona cringed when her father asked for four new cards. Never a good sign! He should have bluffed his way through the hand instead of admitting he had nothing.

As an excellent poker player herself, as well as a tough negotiator in the business world, Fiona saw the clear error in his play. Her father was playing the cards in his own hand. But really good poker players play their opponents' hand. She would have thought that her father was smarter than that, but perhaps he was just too self-centered to think beyond himself.

Father Finn shifted in his chair, elation making him giddy. The cheating bastard was a boon to his plans! He couldn't believe how perfect everything was going! He was in the castle and he could finally search for the damn knife while everyone was distracted by the poker game. Maybe he could find it and get out of town. He'd lost the syringe somewhere between here and town, but he had a new one. So if Fiona, or anyone else, happened to find him searching the house, then he'd just stab them with the GHB concoction and...hell, accidents happened in old houses all the time. A little push down the stairs would fix any wandering eyes.

Of course, if he didn't find the damn knife, he was going to have to go back to plan A, which was kill Fiona so that he'd have more time to search properly.

However, if she was getting married, she would be out of town for her honeymoon. That would be the ideal time to search the castle. So maybe he didn't need to get rid of her if she was finally, *finally*, taking an extended trip! The only reason he'd tried to kill her in the first place was because she didn't ever leave the castle unattended for long enough.

Granted, he rather liked killing. It had given him a thrill the first time. Each time after that, his kills had become more complicated and more enjoyable. However, he didn't want to go to prison because of a mistake he'd made during that first kill. He'd stupidly hidden the knife with his fingerprints on it here in this damn castle!

He played another two rounds, winning one, but losing the second. He was basically staying even, but that was only because he wasn't sitting at the other table. The ante at the other table was outrageous and the participants raised the bets by a thousand dollars or more.

Relieved, he shifted in his seat, preparing to depart.

"Deal me out of the next hand," he called out. No one really paid attention. They were all listening, waiting to hear who won the round at the other table. The chips in the center of the other table were worth well over fifty thousand dollars. Fiona's father was bluffing, again, and everyone at the table knew it. Hell, everyone in the room knew it. They could see it in Duncan's eyes as his gaze darted around the room. If that wasn't a sure giveaway, the sweat dripping down his face was.

Apparently, Duncan wasn't nearly as good an actor as he thought!

He stepped out of the dining room, pretending that he was simply heading for the lavatory. He had no idea where the bathroom was, so that would be yet another excuse to offer if anyone caught him somewhere he shouldn't be.

He pulled out the syringe, keeping it handy just in case. He wasn't sure if it was illegal to search someone's house if he'd been invited in, but he was more concerned with ruining his reputation in the village. If this night's search failed, he needed to maintain his position. If he found the knife, then he could...eh, maybe he'd stick around a bit longer. It was a nice village, with lots of jovial and unsuspecting people he could swindle or murder. A man needed a hobby, after all.

Callum kept his eye on Duncan, but was still relying on Dash and Fiona to watch more closely. He, Marcus, Kasim, and Angela were busy working together to bust the guy's betting pattern. They weren't colluding, but they all focused their attention on beating Duncan. If Callum beat out one of his friends in the process, even better!

Kasim was dealing this round. None of them allowed Duncan to deal. He'd deal from the bottom of the deck and, even though he hadn't stacked the deck, they didn't trust him.

Cards were dealt and Callum picked up his cards. He fought to not react when he saw the three kings in his hand. Three kings!

"I'll take two," he replied, tossing the non-king cards onto the table.

Kasim handed him two more cards. He lifted them up and saw a two, then another two. Damn!

The bidding started. He kept pace with the others, still watching Duncan. The old bastard had only about ten thousand dollars left.

Disgusted with the whole process, he tossed several chips into the pot. "I'll raise it ten thousand." There, that would either put him out of the hand or out of the game. If he agreed with the bet, Duncan would be out of chips.

Callum watched Duncan. He had a good hand. The man wasn't sweating quite as badly as he had been earlier. The question was whether he had better than three of a kind and a pair.

Probably not.

Callum looked over at Marco. He didn't have a good hand. Callum could feel it. Angela? Yeah, she was still in. He could practically see the gears turning in her head, trying to gauge how good his hand was.

Kasim? No clue. The man's expression didn't change no matter what kind of hand he held. However, he tended to tap his fingers. Yep, his "tell" was a finger tapping on his cards when he had something good. No finger tapping at the moment.

Excellent!

That's when Kasim's eyes lifted, glaring at Callum. Kasim slowly smiled, comprehension dawning now, and shook his head.

"I'm out," Kasim announced.

He tossed his cards onto the table. Angela laughed, but she added more chips in. Marco...he looked over at Callum, debating. Something in Callum's face must have warned the other man he was beat. He shook his head and tossed his cards. "Fold," he announced to the table.

It was down to Callum, Angela, and Duncan. "Duncan?" Callum prompted.

The man nodded, shoving his much diminished pile of chips forward. "Don't even try it," the man laughed. "I've got you this time."

Callum tilted his head, considering. Yeah, Duncan had a good hand. That much was obvious. The man didn't have a clue about how to play poker, which seemed odd since he was supposed to be a con man. Even when one had a good hand, it was better to keep it quiet, pretend to bluff until the final reveal.

"Okay, let's see how good your cards are," Callum replied. "Call."

Angela laid out her hand. She had two threes.

Duncan chuckled, shaking his head in a patronizing manner. "No' good enough, darlin'," and he put down his cards. Two aces! Good hand. "I'm back in the game!" he laughed, completely ignoring Callum as he started to reach for the pot.

That's what a good bluffer does, he thought. Kasim snorted, shaking his head. "Not so fast, Duncan." He looked at Callum. "Let's see 'em."

Callum laid out his hand. Three kings sparkled happily in the overhead lighting. The pair of twos wasn't even necessary because the three of a kind definitely beat a pair, even when the pair was higher.

Duncan's jaw went slack. He stared long and hard at the cards, his hands frozen on the table.

"Nay!" he whispered.

The rest of the room went dead silent. He'd lost. He'd lost the hand and he'd lost MacGreggor castle!

The silence was almost deafening.

No one moved. No one even breathed. For a long moment, the air was still.

"Nay!" Duncan roared, leaping to his feet and literally shoving the poker chips, cards, and all, across the table. "Nay!" He turned, ready to leap at Callum. But Dash had anticipated such a reaction, as had Callum. In unison, they stood, moved around the table, and glared at the outraged man.

"I won, fair and square, Duncan."

Color drained from his face. He shrugged off Dash's hand, jerking his clothes back in place. "I will fight you on this!" he snarled.

Callum tilted his head to the side. "That is your right."

Duncan, however, was not as calm. His fury was out of control. He walked a couple of paces, then shoved the candle holders and silver bowl off the sideboard as his rage escalated. The food scattered across the carpet.

"Get oot!" he screamed to the crowd. "Get oot, all o' you! Get oot o' me house!"

Angela stepped closer, the document he'd signed in hand. "You no longer own this house, Mr. Reid."

He stared at the papers, and dove to rip them away. But she stepped out of the way, shaking her head as she tut-tutted his efforts. "Not a good move, Mr. Reid. I think you should consult with your lawyer about the actions you're about to take. These papers have been signed and witnessed. They are valid. I made sure of it."

Duncan glanced at each of them, his fury spiraling higher. "Ye're all cheaters! I'll sue ye fer cheating! Ah can prove it too!"

Angela was calm in the face of his anger. But James, her husband, moved to stand protectively by her side regardless.

Duncan's charm and graciousness had vanished completely. Marco and Callum stepped closer, shaking their heads in disgust. "This isn't going to help, Duncan. Why don't you head down to the pub and have a pint? Calm down and figure out what you're going to do next."

The man bellowed his fury. Those words only seemed to inflame his anger higher and he roared, wild-eyed and beyond words.

Duncan pushed his way through the crowd, shoving furniture until it toppled, clearing the table with a wild swing of his arm. Finally, Marco and Dash stepped forward. Each grabbed one of Duncan's flailing arms and literally lifted him off of the floor to haul him out the door.

Kasim's guards, alerted by the commotion, were rushing towards the front door. Dash and Marco shoved the man outside and the guards instantly took over, slapping plastic cuffs on his wrists.

"Wha' the hell are ye doin'?" Duncan demanded. "Ye canna arrest me! I havna dun anythin' wrong!"

The guards lifted him off of his feet. Kasim said something to them in Arabic and the men nodded, then carried Duncan away. Fiona couldn't see where they took him since Dash and Callum shoved the door closed.

Someone cleared his throat and the group turned to find Bernard standing awkwardly in the doorway. "I think..." he looked over at Fiona. "My dear, there is a bit too much drama in your life. I'm afraid you'll have to find a new beau to court you." And with that, he hunched his shoulders as he hurried out through the front door.

In the ensuing silence, everyone stood in a rough circle, not sure what to say or do. Finally, Rosalee broke the tension. "Good grief!" Rosalee commented, walking over to wrap her arms around her husband's waist. "What a mess!"

A sudden crash sounded from a room behind them and everyone turned as one. Fiona rushed towards the great room, Callum barely a step behind her. They rarely used that room since it was so enormous. But it was beautifully decorated with leather couches situated around the massive stone fireplace. There were other smaller sitting areas as well, and long, velvet curtains graced the windows. The look was finished off by a line of suits of armor standing at attention against one wall, reminding visitors that this truly was a castle that had defended its people from intruders.

Fiona stepped into the room in time to see Father Finn up on his toes, straining to shove something back onto the top shelf of a bookcase.

"Father Finn?" she asked, astonished, everyone crowding into the room behind her. If the evening hadn't already been so wild, the visual of the village priest sifting through her belongings might seem almost comical. Especially when the priest turned to look at her over his shoulder, eyes wide. Unfortunately, another box came loose, dumping its contents all over him.

"Oh goodness!" Fiona gasped. "Those are the boxes that the church asked me to hold onto several years ago!"

She hurried over to kneel down beside the slightly dazed Father Finn. "Were ye trying te get them back?" she asked.

The man stared up at her, his eyes wide. Everyone looked at the old, wooden box that had shattered all over the stone floor, its contents spilling out over the pavers.

A knife?

"Don't touch it!" Josh ordered, stepping carefully over the flood of detritus. "That's dried blood. There may be finger prints."

Fiona was close enough to Father Finn to hear his sharp intake of breath. She started to turn toward him. He lunged forward, grabbing her arm as he stood, dragging her to her feet as well. He wrapped his arm around her neck and she felt a needle press against her throat.

"Stay back!" Father Finn warned.

No one moved. Everyone just stared at the priest.

"What are ye doin', Father?" Fiona asked, fighting back panic. He wasn't choking her. Not yet. But that needle, she had no idea what was in it.

"I'm getting the hell outta here," he announced. "And ye're my ticket."

"Ye're not leaving with her," Callum announced, his voice grim, his jaw tight with fury.

He pressed the needle closer to Fiona's neck. "Stay back, or I'll do it!"

Callum froze. He couldn't risk a glance at Fiona, couldn't handle it if she was terrified. He had to focus on the priest. Well, obviously, he wasn't a priest. At least, Callum seriously hoped he wasn't! The man had a needle against his woman's neck. He'd damned well better not be a priest!

Calmly, he lifted his hands, palms out. "No one is going to stop you if ye want te run. But I wilna let ye take Fiona."

"What the hell do you care?" he demanded. "You just came into town a week ago! Was this your whole point in coming here? Tricking Duncan, the right sod, out of his castle." The priest laughed harshly. "Dinna get me wrong! We're all sick o' listening to the arse pretend to be lord of the manor. Right sick of him, we are!"

Callum gestured to the contents of the box strewn across the floor. "Whatever you were searching for, just take it and go."

Father Finn laughed. "Yeah, right! Ye're just gonna to let me ride off into the sunset, eh?"

Callum shrugged. "We donna give a damn about ye. Just let her go and get on your way."

Fiona felt something deep inside of her shift! She'd finally wrested her precious home out of her father's hands. She would be damned if she would let some fake priest ruin her triumph!

Remembering her self-defense training, she carefully gripped "Father" Finn's wrist and forearm. With her fingers around his wrist, she stepped to the side, shifting her neck away so that the needle didn't poke her harder. With her other hand, she clenched her fist and, with as much power as she could muster, slammed her fist into his unprotected groin. The needle moved away from her neck as Finn's head came down, reacting to the force of her fist. But she wasn't done yet. While his head came down, she slammed her elbow upwards, right into his jaw. Stunned, Finn dropped like a stone, losing his grip on the needle.

Callum grabbed her, cradling her as he ran his hands over her, looking for damage. "Are ye okay?" he demanded. His hands cupped her jaw, tilting her head to the side so he could examine the spot where the needle had pricked her. "Did he get any into ye? Let's get ye te the emergency room." He turned and yelled, "Someone grab that needle! The doctors will need to examine–"

"I'm fine," Fiona whispered. "The needle pricked me, but he didna press down on the plunger."

He stopped, gazing into her eyes. "Are ye *sure*?"

"Positive," she replied, placing her hands on his chest to reassure him.

He groaned and pulled her in for a tight hug. "I love you!" she whispered. "And we're no' going te lose each other now that we've finally found each other."

"I agree," he replied, touching her chin so she looked up at him. "I'm no' going to lose you!"

"You wilna lose me," she whispered back, going up on her toes to kiss him.

Police sirens sounded in the distance and someone must have gone to the front door. Moments later, the police stormed into the room, weapons drawn as they carefully approached Finn, who was still writhing on the floor in pain, even though his hands had been zip tied behind his back.

Josh stepped forward, bagged bloody knife in hand. "I think this was what he was after." He handed it over to the police. "I don't know if there are any unsolved murders in the area, but this might help solve one."

The older of the police officers looked at the knife, then nodded. "Aye, there certainly is an unsolved murder! A couple was killed, stabbed to death, about five years back." The officer eyed Finn in disgust. "I suppose there are fingerprints on this knife that might implicate ye, eh?" he asked, nudging Finn with his foot.

The police lifted Finn up, carrying him out. They then took statements from everyone. It took more than two hours to finish. Meanwhile, Rosalee, Marco, and Chloe went into the dining room to clean up the mess that Duncan had created.

It was well past midnight by the time the castle was settled and everyone had found a bed. There were plenty in the castle since it used to house not just the nobility, but also servants. So it could easily house them all.

But as soon as Callum closed the door to Fiona's room in the east wing of the castle, he knew he wouldn't be able to sleep.

"His name wasna Father Finn. He murdered an elderly couple five years ago. The blood on the knife was theirs and the fingerprints on the knife were from Father Finn. Or whate'er his name was. Apparently, he was masquerading here in the village in order to find that knife," he explained, watching as Fiona brushed her hair in front of an old fashioned dressing table. He put his hands on her shoulders, watching her in the mirror. "The castle is finally yers."

She smiled, then twisted around to face him. "The castle is *yours*, Callum MacGreggor. This was yer brilliant scheme. Ye are now the rightful owner of yer birthright." She kissed him then, putting all of her love into it.

"It's *ours*," he corrected when he lifted his mouth. "You asked me to marry you earlier. And I'm going to hold ye te that promise."

She grinned, her fingers sliding against his bare chest. "I wouldna have it any other way." Her eyes twinkled in the dim light. "Now will you please tell me that you love me again?"

He chuckled softly, then lifted her into his arms, carrying her to the bed. "I love you," he replied. "I love every damn inch of yer stubborn, beautiful body."

They didn't fall asleep until the early hours of the morning. They made love, and talked, and made love some more. Then talked some more, made plans, and made love again.

It was the perfect ending to a truly horrific day. But everything was right in the world now, because Callum loved her!

Epilogue

The flowers were in full bloom as she stepped out into the bright afternoon sunshine. With her pale skin, she couldn't wear white. Instead, she wore an ivory gown with pearls sewn into the bodice and a long, flowing skirt that ended at her ankles. Fiona chose not to wear a full length gown since she wanted to be married in her garden. It was where she'd first met Callum, so it seemed only right to make their vows there.

Walking towards him, she beamed at the awe on his face. But it was the promise in his eyes that caused her pale cheeks to turn that particular shade of pink.

As she took his hands under the arch of flowers, Fiona gave him a look. "I dinna know how ye play poker so well. Ah can read yer thoughts at a glance."

Callum laughed, then bent to kiss her before turning to face the minister. "Maybe it's not *my* thoughts you were reading," he whispered.

If she hadn't been standing in front of a man of faith, she might have said something...irreverent. But since she was, and because this was their wedding day, she refrained.

"Dearly beloved," the minister began. Fiona felt Callum's fingers tighten around hers, silently telling her that he loved her. She squeezed back, sending him the same message. No need to read each other's minds when their body language was so much more accurate.

A message from Elizabeth:

So what did you think? In Marni and Maxine's story, I didn't have enough interaction between the guys and Angela. Did I fix that issue in Staking a Claim? Was it okay?

Any chance you could take a brief moment to leave a review?. If you could just go back to the retailer website that you purchased the book to the review page – and I thank you!

As usual, if you don't want to leave feedback in a public forum, feel free to e-mail me directly at elizabeth@elizabethlennox.com. I answer all e-mails personally, although it sometimes takes me a while. Please don't be offended if I don't respond immediately. I tend to lose myself in writing stories and have a hard time pulling my head out of the book.

Elizabeth

And now…!! A new series – with Yummy Sheiks!! Keep scrolling for a sneak peek at "The Sheik's Marriage Contract" – coming January 13, 2023! (Wahoo!)

Excerpt from "The Sheik's Marriage Contract: Release Date: January 13, 2023

"Who is here?" Tazir snapped, not in the mood to handle anything more today. It was well past the dinner hour and he was exhausted. He wanted to head out to the pool for a swim or maybe go down to the gym for a hard workout. Unfortunately, he was too late to head outside for a hard gallop, but his stallion, Zinz, probably needed the exercise just as much as Tazir did. So whoever had just arrived, asking for a meeting with him without an appointment would have to just buzz off! He wasn't seeing anyone else today!

"A Ms. Lila Chakroun, Your Highness," Eldra, his assistant, explained in a low, calm voice.

Lila? The lovely, spirited girl who used to play with his sisters? The girl who had grown into a gorgeous, stunningly beautiful woman?

"Lila is here?" Rayed interrupted, coming around the corner and looking just as worn out as Tazir. "Lila Chakroun is here? In the palace?"

The assistant bowed again, this time to Rayed. "Yes, Your Highness. Actually, Ms. Chakroun is in one of the guardrooms at the moment. Not exactly inside the palace."

"What does she want?" Tazir demanded sharply.

The man shook his head. "Nothing, Your Highnesses. She simply walked up to one of the guard posts outside on the street and asked how you were."

Tazir's eyes narrowed. "The guard allowed her to enter the building?"

Eldra nodded. "Apparently, someone was harassing her on the street. Ms. Chakroun appeared flustered and anxious. So the guard brought her into the office to protect her while two other guards went out to investigate and question the two men who were bothering her."

Rayed turned and glared at Tazir. "Someone was bothering Lila!" Rayed growled.

Tazir rolled his eyes. "I heard that part." He turned back to his assistant. "Why isn't Lila here in the palace?"

Eldra shook his head. "She does not have an appointment, Your Highness. Nor does she have the correct credentials that would allow her to pass through the security checks. But I recognized her name from years ago. I know that she's distantly related to your former step mother."

"And she's still here?" Tazir demanded.. He turned to his lead bodyguard. "Have Lila brought to my office immediately."

The guard didn't hesitate. He lifted his hand and spoke into the microphone attached to his wrist. He waited for the response from the guardroom, then turned to Tazir. "She's being led through the security room now."

Tazir nodded sharply, then returned to his office. "I'll see her immediately."

Rayed watched his older brother move towards his desk. Tazir had started his morning at four o'clock, having been woken early due to a problem in the northern region. It was now about thirty minutes past seven in the evening, he hadn't eaten dinner, and had probably skipped lunch as well. Tazir was working too hard, he thought. But Tazir wouldn't slow down. Every time he tried, something would happen and he was called back to deal with it.

Rayed took as much off of Tazir's shoulders as possible, but his older brother was too focused on his duties and obligations to release more. The man worked twenty hour days and was constantly exhausted.

But at the mention of Lila Chakroun, his entire demeanor had shifted.

Turning, he focused on Eldra. In a low voice, he instructed, "Tell the palace staff to get a room ready for Ms. Chakroun. And find out where she's living. Send someone to her apartment to pack up her personal items. Make sure it is a woman that packs up Ms. Chakroun's clothing though." He considered the situation for another long moment, then added, "On second thought, don't worry about bringing her clothes here to the palace." Lila probably didn't have clothes in the latest fashion. For what Rayed had in mind, Lila would need to look her best. "Have Marci, our personal shopper, arrange for an entire wardrobe to be delivered here. Assume that Lila will need everything, including makeup."

Suzanne suddenly appeared, her hazel eyes shifting from Eldra to Rayed, sensing a secret. That annoyingly perky smile appeared right on schedule, but there was a tinge of anxiety in her eyes. "What's going on? Someone is getting a new wardrobe?" she asked slyly. "I love Marci's fashion sense! She's so elegant, but with a quirky edge!"

Rayed looked down at the woman, not sure what the hell she was talking about. Ignoring her, he looked at Eldra. "And shoes."

Eldra was writing frantically, but at that last part, he nodded and walked away.

"Ooh! I love shoes too!" Suzanne clapped her hands excitedly.

Rayed started to walk away, but remembered that conniving look Suzanne had aimed at Tazir the last time she'd been in his office. She was planning something, maybe even manipulating events, and Rayed wasn't sure what her plan was. Better to get her out of the way so that Tazir had some private time with the lovely Lila.

"Could you come with me to discuss those wedding plans?" he asked, gesturing down the hallway. "I don't think that Tazir has the time to review them right now. Maybe I should take a look and make sure that there aren't any issues."

Suzanne perked up, but out of the corner of his eye, he saw Antoine roll his eyes. Rayed wasn't sure what that was about, but his primary goal was to clear a path for Lila. There was something serendipitous happening that Lila, Tazir's old flame, showed up on the same day that they'd been discussing wedding plans.

"That would be great! I'd love it if you could give me some insight into Tazir's," at his sharp look, Suzanne corrected herself, "I mean, His Highness' preferences. I really want this to be a spectacular event. And you're right, he's been working so hard lately to..." the woman kept babbling, but Rayed stopped listening. He nodded to his bodyguards, giving the signal to clear the area and keep it that way.

"Oh, thank you but I'm sure that whoever that was is gone now," Lila insisted, lifting her hands to stop the man's insistence that she follow him deeper into the palace.

"Please, come this way, Ms. Chakroun," the short man repeated, more firmly this time.

She shook her head. "No, really! The men who were trying...well, they are gone now," she explained, waving towards the sidewalk in front of the palace. It was empty now and she felt safe enough to hurry down the street to her small townhouse.

Maybe! Perhaps the palace guards had merely scared the goons that had been threatening her further away. Were they waiting for her around the corner? Were they going to pounce on her as soon as she reemerged and spout more dire threats of pain and bodily mutilation?

"Ms. Chakroun?" one of the guards prompted hesitantly.

She turned back to him, glancing at the two guards standing at attention, then back out at the street. No sign of the horrible goons. She hitched her purse higher onto her shoulder and nodded, feigning a confidence that she didn't feel. "I'm fine. Thank you so much for your impromptu rescue. Your team is too kind. But I need to be getting home now. I'm renting a place for the week and I'm just a few blocks away."

Rayed stepped into the guardroom, his height and brawn instantly filling up the space. He looked around until his eyes landed on her. "Lila, please tell me that you're not trying to escape without saying hello!"

His booming voice filled the air and she was startled to see how much he'd grown over the years. "Your Highness!" she gasped. A moment later, she was enveloped into a giant bear hug, literally lifting her off her feet. She laughed, hugging him back, truly thrilled to see him.

When he pulled away, her hands lingered on his shoulders. "You look so great!" she said, beaming up at him. "And wow, you are freakishly tall!"

They laughed together as Lila reclaimed her hands. "Although, I should have known you would be like this," she teased. "You were always taller than me."

He leaned forward, a glimmer of mischief in his eyes. "Remember when we tried playing hide and seek?"

She giggled, delighted at the reminder of those games. "You and Tazir could never find hiding places big enough!" she filled in, as they chuckled at the memory. "Goodness, how *are* you?"

"I'm quite well," he replied, then put a hand to her arm, leading her towards the doorway to the main palace area. "Why are you trying to leave so quickly? We haven't seen or heard from you in years."

Lila flushed at the memories of the last time she'd visited the palace. "I know. I'm sorry I never came back after university." She'd been too overwhelmed by her feelings for Tazir. Feelings she knew couldn't be returned. She'd been a foolish, wishful teenager. But her classes at university had given her the time she'd needed to put her feelings into perspective.

He paused, pulling the door open and leading her down a long hallway. "I understand."

She hesitated, those two words seeming to be more...perceptive...than she'd like. But as usual, his expression gave nothing away. She peered down the hallway hesitantly. "I didn't want to disturb anyone. I was just here to...well, get out of the sun for a minute. It's a hot day."

A dark eyebrow lifted at her statement. "The guards told me you were being harassed by a pair of thugs."

She pulled back, startled that he already knew the details. "No! It was just...a misunderstanding! Nothing important." She reached for the door again. "I really need to get back to work. I have a deadline tonight and..."

"Nonsense. You posted your blog article earlier today and your next blog isn't due for another three days."

Her eyes widened. "You...know about my blog?"

He laughed and nudged her forward. "Of course we know about your blog. Your articles criticizing my economic policies and Tazir's social policies are very influential. We appreciate your candor, even if we don't always agree with you."

She cringed. "Well, I don't just criticize your government policies. I'm an equal opportunity annoyance."

He chuckled easily and nodded. "Your insights into other government policies are brilliant, Lila. You majored in political science, if I recall?"

She looked around suddenly and discovered that they were coming towards the stairs that would lead to the administrative branch of the palace. How had he managed to get her all the way down the hallway? "Yes, but...seriously, I don't want to intrude. I know how hard everyone here works and," she glanced at her watch, noting that it was already late evening. "It's dinner time. I'm sure that Tazir is exhausted."

"Tazir would beat me if I didn't bring you to him." He pushed open the door that led to the larger offices. Despite the late hour, the area was buzzing with people, everyone hard at work. Some were on the phone, others were working at computers, and there were many people rushing down the hallways or weaving their way through the open area desks. There were offices on both sides of the room and the energy was almost palpable.

"I really...!" she gasped, words failing her when he paused outside of a set of familiar double doors guarded by two stern-faced men that didn't look happy to see her. "No. I can't go in there."

"Nonsense," Rayed replied, then pushed open the door and literally shoved her inside. A moment later, the door closed behind her.

Lila stood still, just inside the door. The office was stunning. There was a sitting area with leather sofas and club chairs, a massive desk on the far side of the room and a conference table surrounded by leather chairs. There was a fully stocked bar and...goodness, there he was! Tazir!

He was pouring something into a pair of wine glasses, but Lila barely noticed.

Tazir. He was taller than she remembered. And much bigger! Many more muscles were packed onto Tazir's tall frame. Which was a ridiculous thought since she hadn't seen him in years! Of course he'd grown taller and more muscular!

But he was also harder, more intimidating. And, much to the chagrin of her delicate heart, so much more alluring. The tanned skin, hard jawline, and the five-o'clock shadow made him look almost menacing. Dark hair with just a hint of grey at the temples. Why grey? He was only thirty seven years old!

Those dark, intense eyes watched her for a long moment and she felt the familiar trembling inside of her. It had always been like this. At least, on her side it had been. Tazir was the standard by which she compared every other man. And every single one of them fell short of his standard. Tall, dark, and handsome didn't come close to explaining the appeal of Tazir. He was beyond powerful. Not because of his position as one of the wealthiest, most powerful men in the world. But because...because of him. Because there was a confidence about him, a charisma that pulled her in.

In a word, the man was magnificent. She'd always thought so. She'd had such a painful crush on him during her teen years. He'd been so handsome, so dynamic and amazing. So educated and confident. They'd spent hours debating the issues in the world, laughing at each other's opinions, snorting at their disagreements, and just...generally enjoying the arguments.

That crush was one of the reasons she'd left Fahre. She'd attended Stanford University in the United States instead of choosing one of the celebrated universities here in Fahre.

It was also the reasons she'd stayed away for so many years. Nothing could come of that painful crush. Nothing at all! He would have to marry some day and she planned to be far, far away when that happened.

"Lila." Goodness, the way he said her name sent shivers down her spine!

Made in United States
North Haven, CT
03 April 2024